A Place
And A Time

A Place And A Time

by Barbara Schoen

SCHOLASTIC BOOK SERVICES

New York Toronto London Auckland Sydney Tokyo

For D. R. S.

Contents

1

The Talisman

The hardest day for me has always been each September, the last day before we leave the shore.

Our house is just a summer cottage like a million others, with no heat except the stove and fireplace. The boards and beams show, with nails sticking through, and the whole place smells like wood. Even inside the house you can smell the pine needles. I would know I was there with my eyes shut.

I wouldn't give up a minute at the shore for anyone; I fought each year for every last second. I never wanted to leave the big living room with the driftwood over the stone fireplace and the table scattered with magazines and the couch with the broken spring where I could always sleep. I wished that I would break my leg or get smallpox so they couldn't move me.

The summer that I was fourteen I saw my way to a brief reprieve. The night before we were to leave I asked Mother please could I stay over an extra day with Aunt Anne and Priscilla to help them close the house after everyone else had left for Westchester.

Mother thought it was a terrible idea. She told me that Aunt Anne found me a "difficult" child; Aunt Anne "absolutely abhorred" my "disconcerting habit" of staring at people for a few seconds before I answered them. (Daddy always said that I was taking x-rays of people's souls. It embarrassed people who didn't have any.)

Mother didn't want to leave me at all (and she was so right!), but I pleaded and absolutely promised that I would be a tremendous help if only I could stay that one more day.

Dad said, "Let her. She won't tear up the pea patch. Will you, Josie?"

Mother frowned and said (I didn't get it at the time, but I certainly did the next day) that I simply had to learn to understand and be more patient with people that I found boring and irritating. "Suffer fools," she told me her generation called it. She said it was a matter of dignity, mine and theirs.

How did Mother always know all too well what would happen? I was so undignified that night I could have crawled. But then I had not yet found the talisman, the charm that was to help me be big enough to go on and on and on being kind while they picked and picked and picked on me.

I had my way about staying. In the morning Mother left with Grammy and Paul after an early breakfast, and Dad and Uncle Jack took the first plane. Aunt Anne and Priscilla and I were to drive down as early as we could manage the following day.

As soon as Mother left I started on the bedrooms, bureaus, and closets. I really tidied up. I did my best all day. I nearly died trying. If Aunt Anne had known how grim it was to have to spend my last day indoors, cleaning out kitchen cabinets, putting mothballs in blankets, she never would have cornered me the way she did.

Grammy's room came first. It still smelled of Grammy: warm, a little stuffy, and like lavender. She hadn't put away one single thing! How like her!

Grammy was a queen, to me. She provided a whole dimension in my life. I visited her often in the winter. To get away from my family. (Weekends could turn into pick sessions.) Grammy always had time for me: to go to a movie, to play double solitaire, or just to listen.

I saw that she had left her scrapbooks behind, lying on her marble-topped bureau with the oval mirror. Suppose I hadn't been the one to do her room? What would I have done without them all winter?

I idly leafed through the familiar pages. From the very minute that she and Grandfather met, Grammy saved pictures, telegrams, every important thing in their lives together. I passed my favorite clipping: Grandfather heading up a search party the night Grammy was lost on Mount Washington. He looked frantic but fed up at the same time. Reading the scrapbooks was better than reading a novel, to me. I sat down on Grammy's bed.

3

They were like a love story of Grandfather and Grammy. In the second book the babies came. Aunt Anne. I wished I wasn't named for her. Josephine Ann Frost. At least nobody could make me spell it her way. Who would know Aunt Anne from her scrapbook picture? All chubby smiles and a smooth, unfrowning forehead. And Grammy's eyes sparkling with the joy of her. Dad's baby picture. And a precious wisp of hair from the little one that didn't live.

I heard some banging in the hall outside Grammy's door, so I stood up and pretended to dust the leather covers while I turned the pages of happy years quickly until I came to the few pictures of Grandfather in his uniform before he went overseas. Grandfather took most of the pictures, so after his plane went down in 1943 there weren't any more for a long time. In fact there were no entries of any kind.

I skipped quickly over the glossy, professional photographs of Aunt Anne and Uncle Jack's wedding. And (if you'll pardon the expression) Baby Priscilla.

Daddy and Mother's wedding.

Yes! The adorable pictures of cute Baby Josie! And passable ones of little brother Paul.

Kodachrome prints, not pasted in, fluttered to the floor. Grammy and Dad and me in the sloop; Mother and Aunt Anne and Priscilla in the kitchen; and a really sickening one of Priscilla showing off on her everlasting water skis. I stuck that one upside down in the back of the book so that no one would have to have the unpleasant experience of running across it.

"Josie?"

I looked up, quick with guilt. Aunt Anne stood in the doorway. She hadn't noticed what I was doing.

"How are we coming, child?" she asked. She was wearing stretch slacks and a scoop-necked knit blouse. She did her hair in a smooth puff, but it always looked kinky when we were at the shore because of the salt air. I thought, what a stupid way to dress and what a stupid way to do your hair!

"Fine, thank you, Aunt Anne," I answered politely.

"Well, don't spend too long in Grammy's room, dear. She should have done it herself," said Aunt Anne, leaving me again.

I piled the scrapbooks near the door so that I would remember to take them with me. More than anything I wished that I could curl up on Grammy's big four-poster bed with its white candlewick bedspread and pull up the fluffy wool blanket and doze, as I so often did. But instead I stripped the bed and put the blankets into a plastic case with mothballs and pushed on to Paul's room.

There I chucked out all the broken seashells and poor dried-up hermit crabs and shriveled seaweed that he had cherished so. On my windowsill there was a paper cup of black-eyed Susans that he brought back from his last trip to the meadow. I couldn't throw them out, but Priscilla didn't have any trouble doing it. I wished we didn't have to share a room.

Priscilla was fifteen, almost a year older than I, but that wasn't the only difference. Priscilla was the kind of girl who wore white sandals with a rubber daisy sticking up between her toes, instead of sneakers. And white shorts (short, that is), not jeans or Bermudas. Priscilla was what Aunt Anne called "pleasingly plump" (laugh here) so she really looked a sight when she squirmed those big hips of hers into the minute clothes that she and Aunt Anne liked to buy. She was quite nearsighted, but she was too vain to wear her glasses so she missed a lot that went on. When she did wear them they were white and slanty-eyed, with an excess of rhinestones.

Everywhere she went she carried a little transistor radio, cha cha cha. (All summer it was the thing to say cha cha cha after everything.) One time Dad took her sailing with us and she brought the radio and listened to what she called music. (He loves me. He adores me. Twang, twang. Chills, thrills, and vibrations.) So she wouldn't be bored on the boat. I heard Dad tell Mother that after a while the only music we heard was Priscilla hollering when the boat heeled over. Mother asked me did I laugh. When I got to thinking about it I realized I shouldn't have.

I thought that day how you really can't ever be friends with someone who's afraid of the things you like best. Like Priscilla was afraid of the boat heeling over and of going out in the dark. Darkness was my comfort, and racing around the bay with the lee rail under was duck soup to me. But things that made me so scared I felt sick, like going to a dance, or even a Teen Center party, to Priscilla were a wee glimpse of heaven itself.

Priscilla was dying to get back to the boys, boys, boys. She thought that if she slaved away all day and fussed at me every second, we might get going about two and a half minutes earlier the next morning so that we could get home before the pool closed. Imagine wanting to leave the bright, lovely bay to swim in the sickly, chlorine-green pool!

She was an irresistible target. Every time I noticed that she was watching me I would deliberately drag along. Then she'd yell at me and run tell Mums on me. It was just like pushing a button.

With Aunt Anne, when your job was done you didn't get to go. You were supposed to stand around and see what was next to do. That was the way Miss Prissy did. Aunt Anne had her well trained. (Like a circus poodle.) I even watched her tell Priscilla which leg of the table to dust first.

In the afternoon I did kitchen shelves, and the sun got lower and lower and began to make pointed shadows out of the fir trees, and I knew the last day was slipping away from me. Through the window I could see the blue line of ocean edged with browning salt grass and goldenrod; and even if I didn't want to I had to think of tomorrow, when the slanting rays of the late afternoon sun would fall on no one, only on emptiness and gathering dust.

But I kept on going and I talked to myself the way I sometimes have to, and I said, "Josie, hang on for a few more hours. After dinner you'll be free." That was what Aunt Anne said. "Let's get it all done, girlies. So that we can enjoy our last evening." And I thought how it would be at the shore at nine o'clock when the tide was just high, and I felt that I could wait.

We did finish before dinner. Was I relieved! At first I thought we'd have a sandwich and then I could go. When everyone is at the shore no one notices me; the grown-ups are always having drinks and I slip in and out. I thought it would be like that.

But then Aunt Anne said since this was our Last Night at the Shore we should have a little celebration. She and Priscilla changed their clothes, as though there was someone there to see them. (Bone was the big color that year.) I didn't change and Aunt Anne looked at me, but she didn't say anything.

So then Aunt Anne said didn't we really think she "deserved" a drink? And she thought it would be "congenial" if Priscilla and I had tomato juice. (Priscilla horsed around and said couldn't she have an itsy-bitsy-witty-boo drink, and they went through *that* routine.)

Naturally it ended up that I had to get the tomato juice (as if I even wanted the stuff in the first place) because I had done the kitchen shelves. "And Josie, dear, do be sure it's one of those lit-tle cans. We don't want to have leftover problems." I might have been able to figure that out for myself; nothing makes you madder than to have someone tell you to do something you're going to do anyway. I'd had a whole day of it.

It was hot and stuffy in the living room. A clutter of pillows and knitting wool and cigarette smoke. Aunt Anne asked a lot of picky questions about school. Why did she have to mention it? No one knew how I dreaded the endless winter. She told me how well Priscilla did her sophomore year. She asked why didn't I knit and she said that Priscilla did lovely work (I never saw any of it). I had to hold her hot, prickly yarn.

No matter where the conversation started it would come around to boys. They were one thing I preferred not to think about because I didn't know what to think. Everything was changing from the way it had always been.

Dinner went on forever. Priscilla was eating up a storm. I had my back to the clock and I kept turning around to look. Finally Aunt Anne asked, "Child, what *is* your difficulty?"

Priscilla said, "Tee hee hee. Josie must have a late date. Cha cha cha." And they ran that one to the ground. If Priscilla knew that I was going to the shore after dinner, she'd have thought for sure that I was meeting someone. She'd never have understood that all I hoped to find was myself.

I couldn't manage to eat any dessert (which brought on the usual comments about me being underweight, "just skin and bones" — why didn't they make a tape of it?). I couldn't eat because Aunt Anne kept talking and talking about this intolerable dancing

9

school that she had gotten me into: Miss Hackley's. She told us that she was anxious for Priscilla and me to have all the "advantages." Miss Hackley's was supposed to be an "advantage." You had to wear white gloves. And the coming winter, since I was fourteen, I was to have the tremendous advantage of going to three dances called Get-Togethers. They were neatly spaced to cast a pall over all three vacations: Thanksgiving, Christmas, Spring. (One of them, it turned out, cast a pall over far more than a vacation. It nearly cast a permanent pall over poor little Josie.)

Aunt Anne discussed the Get-Togethers interminably because (oh joy!) she was "on the committee." And she was "all set up" because she had already "managed an escort" for Priscilla. His name was Henry Bassett and he was some kind of second cousin of Uncle Jack's. I tried to look interested while she and Priscilla amused themselves figuring out whether he was "once-removed" or "twice-removed." By the end of dinner I could have drawn the family tree back to Adam and Eve.

It was only September and already I dreaded the Thanksgiving dance (which was two whole months away) so much that it was giving me a stomachache. I was positive that it was going to be the worst night of my whole life. How was I to get through it?

Aunt Anne couldn't stop talking about it. She said she hoped Mother would get me something more "suitable" to wear this year. She hardly thought I could "get away with a cotton" any longer. Although, of course, I couldn't "take" anything too "busy." Maybe a "little velveteen" like Priscilla's.

Even though I was tired, I couldn't sit quietly. My legs were so restless they hurt. But I answered everything nicely and quickly. If we hadn't been about through I couldn't have stood it. I waited and waited to be excused.

Even when we were finished with dessert Aunt Anne went on about how she hoped I was planning to "do something" with my hair (which was straight with long bangs that Dad said I used to hide behind). And it was pick a little, talk a little, pick, pick, pick, until I was actually shaking as though I were cold.

But I knew that sooner or later she had to let me go. Finally, after about a hundred cigarettes, Aunt Anne got up. She said she thought demitasse in the living room would be agreeable while she got her strength up for the dishes. Believe it or not, Priscilla pulled herself together and made the instant coffee because she was allowed (thrills!) to have some. She loaded it with sugar and slurped it down with her little finger sticking out and all her jangling silver bracelets clanking on her wrists. Aunt Anne had the same, but gold. And they both knew how to keep those bracelets moving.

When Priscilla came back I got up and started clearing the table.

"I'll wash up," I said, "while you two enjoy your coffee."

I'd reached the point where I couldn't sit another second — I was nearly out of my mind with boredom and irritation. Picking up a stack of dishes, I headed for the kitchen. I figured I'd finish and slip out the back door.

"Child, you are too sweet," said Aunt Anne. "But I can't let you. Not on your last night. We'll do them together."

Oh, no, I thought. Another half hour!

"I have a surprise for my good girls," Aunt Anne went on, bustling into the kitchen with a platter. Pat pat waddle pat. "I thought we'd have a little Last Night party. Mae will be over any minute now to make a fourth for bridge."

I couldn't believe it.

She just casually dropped this *bomb*.

"Bridge!" I said, loud and astonished.

"We won't play for money, sweet," she soothed. "We know you haven't had much experience."

It was as if Dad remarked, offhand, "Oh, by the way, Josie, we sold the sloop yesterday. We knew you wouldn't mind."

"Bridge!" I repeated. I couldn't keep my voice from sounding frantic. I backed toward the screen door.

"What is it, child?" asked Aunt Anne. She held out one hand to me, cautiously, as though I were a wild animal. In her mind, I knew, were rising shades of two-year-old Josie, Tantrum Queen of the Sandbox Set.

I stared at her until her face became a pinkish-gray blur. But I was getting together a thought about what Mother said: about fools and dignity, and it seemed worthwhile trying to make ends meet.

I could have managed, too, except that right then Priscilla swung around sideway on her chair and began to observe us closely. Almost as though she was expecting to learn something useful.

Aunt Anne noticed. It always upset Aunt Anne to have Priscilla see that she couldn't handle me. Maybe she was afraid it would give Priscilla some ideas. At any rate, Aunt Anne frowned and began to close in on me.

"You'd better stop that at once, Josephine!" she said, using her familiar no-monkey-business voice. "You're being infantile!"

Infantile, I really wasn't. But I still couldn't speak.

"Answer me!" she commanded.

Priscilla giggled nastily.

I exploded. "I'll be damned if I'll play bridge!" I shouted.

"Oh, oh. *Naugh*-ty girl!" said Priscilla.

"You impos-sible child!" said Aunt Anne. "You'll jolly well play bridge if I say so!"

I hardly heard them. "You can't make me!" I shouted. "You aren't my mother!"

"She is for today, dear, cha cha cha," said Priscilla, calmly lapping up the last sticky-icky-sweet drops from her cup. "Josie has to do what Mums sa-y-ays. Can't you make her, Mums?" she goaded her mother.

"I've had all I can stand!" I yelled at her. "And I'd cut my throat sooner than spend my last evening with you, you BIG FAT FOOL!"

My voice was shaking and I couldn't go on. I slung the dishes on the counter and slammed out the screen door. It went bam-slam-bam behind me. And I ran down the back steps under the oak tree where there was no light for them to see me. I stood panting with my hand on the rough bark. It was cool and the darkness protected me. Beyond the safe circle of the dipping branches the moon made the meadow cold-white and bright.

I could see them with their heads together in the yellow light of the stuffy living room, talking about me, most likely, and my problems and how Priscilla didn't have any. (Though Dad always did say that Aunt Anne and Priscilla were each other's biggest problem.) And the all-too-scandalous things that Mother had done wrong. Hashing it over made them feel closer together, cozy and righteous and secure.

I felt alone out under my tree, but it wasn't at all the kind of aloneness that I'd been looking forward to so, through the long, long day.

The brightness of the moonlight blurred. The katydids were singing desperately and the sweet smell of mown hay came up from the meadow behind the house. I couldn't see, but I knew it was the harvest moon. I thought, to me September is the saddest moon. It has the full September tide.

After a while I wiped my eyes and said to myself, "Josie, in the morning when it's time to go they just won't find you."

I felt better and I kicked off my sneakers and I ran under the arch of oaks to the road and downhill along the tar until I came to the ruins of the beach house. I was breathless when I reached the porch. Then, down the rickety passage between the dressing rooms, and I was there.

It was my own place. And mine alone.

In front of me I saw the silver-black bay

and the great moon hanging in the sky above it and the white path of light shining straight to my feet. My roadway! Where it went I went, and they couldn't follow.

I threw my head back and my searching arms up high and my spine prickled the way it does for Beethoven's Ninth when they begin the singing, and I knew how a dog feels when it yowls out loud at the moon.

I couldn't stand it any longer. It was too much. I almost had to look away. I sat down and took the deepest breath that I have ever taken.

From the boardwalk in front of the dressing rooms there are five broad wooden steps. The flood tide washed the bottom step, where I was sitting, just gently. There was no wind, only the lap-slap-lapping of wavelets against the weathered wood.

Early in the summer, in June, the sweetness of the privet floated down from the shore, but in September there was only the bitter smell of salt and kelp.

On the left, maybe twenty feet away, the stone jetty loomed rough and tall, so that I couldn't see over it. The moon cast a shadow there, making the water black and evil and frightening. I shivered to look at it. To the right the beach curved around in cold white light. Behind the beach were black trees and a rising hill and houses with yellow lights and more hot living rooms.

"What could I have done tonight?" I asked myself.

I could have said, "Aunt Anne, I can't play bridge because I have to go down to the shore to see how beautiful the moonlight looks on the bay for the last time until next summer, which seems about a hundred years away right now."

The worst thing wasn't that I'd have sounded like an absolute and complete creep in front of Priscilla; the worst thing was that Aunt Anne would have said, "Child, what a *sweet* thought!" Jingle jingle. Clank clank. "We'll *all* go. We'll walk off our dessert. Run for my sweater." The bone-colored one, of course. And it would have been yattatta, yattatta, yattatta, accompanied by the so-called music on the transistor radio (in case Priscilla got bored) all the way to the beach and back.

How could I have listened to them while I looked at the thing I could not bear to leave, which was the water? From what source came such patience with fools?

I had sailed and swum, June, July, August, September, in the same waves that were running in and out, carrying pebbles and bits of emerald seaweed across my bare feet. As I watched, one wave brought in a single stone, perfectly round and most pure white. I held it and it seemed as though the moon itself had fallen from the night sky into my asking hands.

The stone was to keep, through the whole long winter. It would contain for me: How the sky was deep blue that night with a few bright stars, and the water was darker blue, but not black, with the stripe of white moonlight and little patches of moving flashes on either side where waves lifted and fell. The harbor beacon was an ebony pyramid, crowned with a sparkling ruby, and the channel markers, nuns and cans, were dark on top of the water, making a safe pathway into the harbor. The black hull of a skiff made a cutout against the road of light. To hear, there was only the soft wash of the still-rising tide and the sound was like sleep to me.

At that moment I could have suffered any-one.

Another person sitting there would be look-ing at the exact same thing. It made me wonder if beauty was actually in the place or if it was something that got into the person who was looking.

A grown-up would say, "My, what a pretty night," and then go home. For a grown-up it isn't separate any more. They don't need it the same way. It becomes part of the whole big jumble. Even Mother wouldn't have her mind all on it, because she hadn't done the dishes. Part of her keeps thinking about the dishes. Part of her even goes on talking to Aunt Anne. She had to learn that. She told me.

Any time I was sad or upset or wanted to think about a person I saved it all day until I could be at the beach house. It was the only place where I was my true self. (I turned the white sphere between my fingers.) Because the shore is a place that has always been. It would never change. The things they pushed at me weren't as important; they just weren't important. But I needed to be at the shore to know that.

What could I do to take it with me?

Maybe once you get the knowing of a place and a time inside you so that they are a part of you, then you can keep on talking to the fools and still not lose the feeling.

Maybe once you've listened to the Emperor Concerto a thousand times, you can stand to listen to it with the bedroom door open and answer politely when someone calls and not lose the music.

Maybe when I've read ten thousand books, I'll be able to come to the dinner table after I've been reading and not be "sullen and withdrawn," but smile and talk pleasantly to whoever is there and not lose the person I was in the book.

Or clean kitchen cabinets on the last blue-sky-and-sunshine, sweet-meadow-grass, dark-pine-tree, and moonlight-on-the-water day and not so disgracefully act as though I was losing the whole summer.

When beauty gets to be a part of you, I thought, maybe then you can be big enough to offer dignity to other people. The thing I had to learn was to carry the essence with me, like a charm. To help me suffer them gladly.

For a little bit I sat without thinking, holding my stone, my charm, my talisman. The moon overhead saw a bedraggled, naughty child, shivering and cold, in soppy jeans.

Then I knew what I had to do.

I got up and left the bright bay and went where the trees were black ahead of me toward the yellow lights of the house. Through the window I saw that they were playing canasta. No doubt they had told Mae how I blew and had hashed it all over so thoroughly that even Priscilla was satisfied.

Going into the house wasn't all that easy,

with Priscilla sitting there enjoying the floor show, giving Mae the big wink. But I walked into the living room (stopping to put my sneakers on first), and my voice was firm as I slid into the fourth chair at the card table, and I tried not to stare and hesitate before I spoke.

I said (fingers encircling the stone), "Aunt Anne, I'd like to apologize for being so rude to you" — steady — "and Priscilla. It was inexcusable. I'll be glad to play bridge."

When we left the shore the next morning the stone went with me. I looked out the car window and planned how I would keep it in my pocket or desk during the winter and hold it when I needed to.

In a way it had already worked like a charm. Holding it while I apologized, I'd had a new idea. While Aunt Anne dealt out the first round of cards, I suddenly understood that, after her own fashion, she had done her best to be kind and helpful and nice.

Hope mingled with despair as I watched the familiar summer landscape recede. There were even things to look forward to: Mother had promised we'd redecorate my room, there would be basketball games, my birthday —

I sat a little forward on the car seat and whispered to myself, almost cheerfully, "It might even fit inside a white glove."

2

I Wouldn't Dance
That Way with
Just Anyone

October and November never went so fast. I ruined the whole fall anticipating the Thanksgiving dance. I couldn't eat or sleep, worrying about those terrible four hours.

The dance wasn't supposed to start until nine thirty, but we went early because Mother and Aunt Anne were chaperoning. Aunt Anne was on the committee and had to see about the arrangements. It was at this club, so we all drove over together. Mother and Aunt Anne sat in front; Priscilla and I were jammed into the back with a crummy boy who lives on her block.

I wished I liked Priscilla; it would have been so convenient to like a first cousin. But I couldn't stand her. She was only ten months older than I, but she'd been boy-crazy since Year One.

Going to a formal dance was like going to

the guillotine, to me. If Dad were home, I thought, he wouldn't make me go, but he was away so much during the week, even vacation week. I sat in a cold sweat, a captive audience of one, while Priscilla and Aunt Anne made happy girl-talk.

Priscilla opened with, "Mums, I just a *teensy* bit wish we'd decided to wear my 'Pink.'" (Can't you see them both in it, I thought.) She fussed at the frills on what Aunt Anne calls her "bezooms."

So Aunt Anne said (after *lengthy* consideration), "Dearest Sweet, indeed I do believe The Pink 'brings you out' a little more."

Mother made a funny noise in her throat. Priscilla "developed," as they say, early, and one thing she didn't need was to be "brought out" any further.

From clothing they modulated smoothly into the subject of Priscilla's "man." (Even though I hated the crummy boy, I thought it was despicable to talk as though he weren't in the car at all.)

We had to hear Priscilla chatter on about Heartthrob Henry, Second Cousin Extraordinary. I wished at that moment that he was a thousand times "removed." Aunt Anne gave us the big news that he came from Denver. "They are sending him East to school. So Jack feels we must *do* something about him."

That was how she got her claws into him. She roped him into going to all three dances, the same way she did me.

She went on about how he had spent one weekend with them in October and of course he would have taken Thanksgiving with them except that some . . . umm . . . er . . . school friend had invited him or something. She was rather vague. But he *would* meet them at the dance. And he *was* a real Brain. (Flutter. Flutter.) And he *was* older. (Chills. Thrills.) And he *did* have his own car.

"So why didn't he drive you?" I muttered.

"Jo-sie!" Mother warned.

There was a silence, brief but leaden. Aunt Anne dug out first, burbling on about how well she knew his mother and how she "managed the First Dance" for Priscilla (it was all so fake) and she was certain that he would be very "attentive" all evening, and he surely planned to give Priscilla the Last Dance.

Aunt Anne always says that everyone should be "on the floor" for the Last Dance. It used to give me a picture of a mass temper tantrum, everyone flopping around, kicking and screaming. That was the only kind of Last Dance I could see myself doing with any pleasure.

I could stand listening to just so much and then I had to look out the window. I wished myself away to the September shore. A big yellow street light had just turned itself into the golden harvest moon when the crummy boy (whose head came about up to my shoulder) poked me in the ribs and said, "Whatsay, Josie? Got your rock in your handbag tonight? Or is it in your coat pocket?"

My face got all red. "I don't know what you are talking about," I said to him through my teeth, and the words were like icicles.

He knew I had the stone. He was the one

who snatched it from my desk at school and passed it on to another boy, and another, like a crazy game of keepaway, until it rolled to rest under the radiator in the dust and fluff.

The stone had become, to me, truly the essence (the way a poem could be sometimes) of a place and a time and the person I was capable of being. With me I kept the deep blue sky, a few bright stars, the path of moonlight to my feet.

I had learned that the presence of such beauty was not equally important to everyone; but I also knew there must be, somewhere, other people who needed to carry stones.

I moved my beaded handbag over to the window side of me so that there couldn't be any dirty business from the creep.

He noticed. "What-say we loosen up a bit tonight, Miss Stuck-up?" He thought "what-say" was too smooth for words. "What-say you give it all you've got for a change?" I knew he was raising his eyebrows up and down suggestively. "Try joining the rest of the human race," he said, squirming so close that I could smell the glop on his hair.

"Why don't you stop using that gicky stuff?" I said, pulling pointedly away from him, toward the window.

"Ha ha ha!" he laughed, forced and raucous. "Josie made a joke!" (He's known me a hundred years and he knew exact-ly how to bait me.) He slapped his stupid knee.

"Where were you when they were handing out brains?" I sneered.

"Boys will never like you if you talk to them

like tha-at," Priscilla simpered sweetly.

"How much farther is it?" asked Mother. She sounded a little tense.

"Boys will never like you if you dance like an old broomstick," mimicked the creep, in a high voice.

"He's absolutely right," said Priscilla, fake-friendly. "Really, Jose, you wouldn't have half such a terrible time getting boys to dance with you if you'd remember that you are there to give boys a good time. Ri-ight, Mums?"

"Child, I do believe we might be the wee-est bit of help to Josie," said Aunt Anne. "If we have any extra —"

Mother was starting to breathe hard.

"Mums and I would be so happy to help Josie get started," said Priscilla, "but Josie will have to —"

"Josie will have to learn to be herself," Mother interrupted, roughly. "That's all. But the thing I can't understand —"

"All right, Mother," I said. "That's enough."

What Mother knew and was going to say was that I can dance right along with the best of them. Really shake loose if I feel like it. I practice at home in front of my bedroom mirror. I wear an enormous yellow bath towel and I turn on my newest record full blast. I usually start with a slow stomp and a shade of a shimmy and I work my way to whirling up a real tornado until Dad or Mother hollers quits.

But I wouldn't dance that way with just *any*one. I couldn't imagine doing that in public, with that revolting, sweaty-palmed brat who sat beside me.

24

I tried not to care what they said. I leaned my forehead against the cold glass and looked out the window at the trees that were bare November skeletons and wished that I lived where there were no dances, a place where I could see blue water, with the harbor beacon an ebony pyramid crowned with a flashing ruby, and the channel markers, silhouettes, making a safe pathway for the homebound ships —

It was a long ride, but still we got there too soon. We went through an enclosed porch into the coat room. When I got my coat off I was cold on the top half and warm on the bottom half. I was too skinny for that kind of dress; I'd have given anything for a sweatshirt. It was embarrassing to have boys look at me. I hunched up my shoulders and Priscilla threw hers back. Aunt Anne bustled off to the kitchen. Mother patted my arm. "Just be yourself," she whispered. "It won't last forever." She hurried after Aunt Anne.

But sometimes right now can be forever. The biggest fool in Westchester County couldn't have felt any worse than me, Josie, standing all alone in the middle of the empty dance floor. Priscilla was no help. She grabbed the crummy boy, to "use" him to "get started." I could think of a word for her, but it wasn't the kind you say out loud.

I took cover in the ladies' room. There were some girls in there that I knew, but they weren't acting the usual way. They were acting the boys-way. If I said something ordinary like, "I thought the math was cinchy," they'd say, "Oh, Josie," and they'd titter this high little titter.

Everyone was wearing lipstick but me. Mother suggested it, but I said, "I won't." I wished Mother had made me. It would have been easier for me. I thought, she shouldn't give in so easily.

The ladies' room was like a Degas of the ballet girls. All the girls leaning over the basins at the mirrors or fussing with each other's clothes and hair. I felt like a younger sister. The high little laugh went on and on. I sat down on the chair, the white one that the attendant uses.

Suddenly the music started. There was a squash of rustling crinoline and net at the door. Laughter. Loud music when the door opened. Quiet when it shut. Loud. And quiet.

I looked at my watch. It was nine forty-five. I imagined Priscilla on Cloud Nine by this time, dancing that big First Dance with Henry from-the-lovely-family Bassett. And Aunt Anne with her Royal Merger smile. Maybe whispering to Mother (behind her hand — couldn't let the family down in public), "Where on earth has Josephine got to? I can't *place* her." And Mother (a little worried), saying, "I don't know" (but she could probably make a pretty accurate guess). "She must be *some*where." Actually I was sorry about the Mother-aspect of the whole thing. I hated to see her suffer.

I wished that I had brought a book, but at least there was somewhere to sit. There wasn't always.

I wished that I was a little kid again, like

Paul. They had it easy. There were a lot of things they didn't even know about.

Two more hours to go.

The music stopped and the door opened and in walked Miss Priss and another girl that I knew.

"Jose," squealed Priscilla. "Are you all right? You weren't on the *floor*." That, of course, was the living end, in her book.

I fussed with my stockings. (I was the only person I knew that was so skinny she had to pull her garter belt *up*.) It was getting harder and harder to pretend that I didn't give-a-damn if nobody danced with me all evening. Especially with Princess Priss showing off fancy steps all over the powder room.

The girls started to leave and then Priscilla turned back. She studied me. "Ready?" she said. "Cha cha cha?"

It was so kind of her I almost wept. I told myself, "Josie. How do you think anyone can ask you to dance if you hole up in the ladies' room all evening?" And I got up and followed.

Near the drums we saw three boys that we knew from school. Priscilla and the other girl giggled and smirked at the boys. I didn't crack a smile. I never saw less to laugh about in my whole life.

One of the boys sat near me in Latin II. He was always nice and friendly and he talked to me about his dog, once, when we were working on a passage about dogs in ancient Rome. He told me how the Romans used to have little signs on the doors that said, *"Cave canem."* Beware the Dog. Just the way we have today.

It made Latin more real to me than Caesar dragging his tents and legions all the way to Gaul and back. He had translated the Latin passage into English poetry and I thought that it was very good. He was easy to talk to, really *he* did most of the talking. I remembered that his name was Peter.

The boys started toward us, but one of them nudged his friends and dropped away. Peter recognized me. He was going to ask me to dance! My stomach unknotted. I took a quick triumphant look around the room to see if I could spot Mother and Aunt Anne.

"Oh, *thank* you. I'd *adore* it!" I heard. Priscilla slipped in between me and Peter. She dropped her handbag into his pocket and snuggled up. "Isn't this band absolutely *every*thing?" She sparkled. He smilingly shrugged and whirled away.

Couples were dancing all around me. I didn't know what to do.

Looking hard at the floor, I walked past the stag line. The crummy boy deliberately turned his back on me and began to whisper to a friend.

I thought if I went over to one of the hostesses and talked to her like mad about how nice the decorations looked and how the band was really tops, it would look as though I was so fascinated that I didn't feel like dancing.

I said, "How do you do?"

At first she didn't say a word. Then she patted my cheek and smiled a gooey smile and said (just like Aunt Anne), "Child, how sweet of you to speak. But don't waste your precious party time on me, dear." She practically pushed me away. I saw her whispering and looking at me. You could bet that Item Number One on the next Newscast was going to be a droll saga about how no one would dance with little old Josie.

All that was left was the agony in the ladies' room again.

As I walked I planned how I would sit there on the white chair. In between dances, as the other girls came in, I would duck into one of the stalls and sit it out (so to speak) until the music started again. As I opened the door I was thinking how there were only two fixtures and I was going to create a terrific traffic jam by tying up one for the whole —

"Can I help you, dearie?" The voice belonged to a white-uniformed attendant. Owner of the chair.

"Oh! No!" I said. Panicked, I went into one of the stalls and leaned against the wall.

I couldn't go out on the dance floor again. No one could. Even holding tight to my stone, my charm, my talisman, I couldn't stand there all evening in front of Aunt Anne and Priscilla while no one asked me to dance.

I flushed the toilet a couple of times.

It would take a whole rock pile of round stones to screw that much courage to the sticking place. My eyes started to sting. *Now cut that out!* I told myself.

"Everything all right in there, dearie?" asked the woman.

"Hotsy totsy," I managed.

The thing to do was to go out and sit in the car. There was a rug in the back seat. Anyway, November wasn't really that cold. I could come back in just before the last dance.

I came out of the john and looked in the mirror at my long brown hair, unstylishly fluffy at the ends. Mother was always saying that I had the kind of hair I *could* do something with. Why hadn't I?

"Pretty!" said the attendant.

I looked hideous. Dragged out. Ghastly white with owl eyes. I knew she was angling so I'd drop a quarter in the saucer, already primed with small change. Priscilla always clanked some in, to show she'd been around. I couldn't stand it, the sickening way she had of being too-too girlie-friendly with every bathroom attendant she ran into. I was sure Miss Priss must be having an everlasting ball with Henry the Big-Brain Bassett being madly attentive all over the floor. I wondered what the attendant would do if I snatched the change and ran.

I took a penny (Canadian) from my bag and dropped it in the saucer. "Thank you," I said, haughtily, and marched out.

I proceeded toward the front door, thinking, if Aunt Anne or Mother stops me, I'll say that I'm going to the coat room to get something out of my coat pocket. But no one did stop me and I reached the front door unobserved.

Then I noticed, off to the right, a long enclosed porch, unused in winter. It was warm and dimly lighted from the dance floor, and it extended around the corner of the building. Blessed privacy was just around the bend. My eyes flooded with the relief of it. I opened my bag for a handkerchief, turned the corner and —

"Oh, no!" I gasped, startled into dropping my open bag.

Alone, on a sheet-covered rattan chair, sat a boy.

"I'm so sorry!" I blurted. "I didn't know —" I snatched at my bag. My heel caught in the hem of my dress and threw me off balance.

"Oh!" I said helplessly. I watched the contents of the bag spill onto the floor. "Oh, dear me!" My stone was rolling away and the boy was watching it. I stuffed everything else back in, higgledy-piggledy. Across the sloping floor the stone rolled, right toward him. "Oh, please." I held out my hand.

He fielded it like a shortstop.

"Don't throw it!" I said.

I saw that he wasn't going to. He sat back again and examined it, curiously. It came to rest in the palm of his hand.

I wasn't sure if he was teasing some new way. "May I please have my stone back?" I pleaded, shrilly. I was shivering. I wanted to run, but I wasn't going to leave without it.

His fingers curled around it.

"Cuttyhunk?" he asked.

He looked directly at me for the first time, and I saw that he had serious eyes in a friendly face.

"What do you mean?" I asked.

"Cuttyhunk. An island off Connecticut. The seaward beach is famous for perfect stones like this. The waves make them. Under certain specific physical conditions."

I started to say that I got it in Maine, but he went on talking.

"A sphere has some special physical properties," he said. "Did you know that it has the least possible exposed surface area for its mass?"

I tried to look intelligent. "You mean it's all sort of pulled in on itself," I said. It seemed rather clever of the sphere. I brooded about it.

"It must depend on the period of oscillation of the basin," he interrupted, "but I've never found such a one as this. You have something unique." He stared at it, almost into it, as though it were a crystal ball. Hypnotized by its perfect roundness. "We stopped at Cuttyhunk last summer," he continued. "Dad and I chartered a ketch. Thirty-five feet over-all. Sit down."

I plumped down on the edge of another sheet-draped chair.

"Looking at it . . . makes me remember —" he said, turning the stone over and over, as if to derive some magic from it. "One night I took my sleeping bag on deck, before school started. It was so bright. The moon was a perfect sphere . . . like this." He rotated it with his fingertips, reluctant to return it. "Seeing this . . . makes me almost —" He looked at me, I thought, to see if I was laughing at him. But I wasn't. "— makes me almost *be* there. Instead of at this —" he shrugged his shoulders, "— dance," he finished, lamely.

He wasn't too good at words. They came out jerky and halting, but I could see how it had looked to him. It was as though we were looking with the same eyes.

"You can hold it if you want to," I said. I wasn't worried any more.

"All around, when I looked up . . . the masts and spars made black lines."

"A black lattice against star-sprinkled sapphire," I added, to help him.

"It was so bright I could read the tag on my sleeping bag," he said. "It's the best bag. Real down. Good to minus thirty Fahrenheit."

"There was a path of moonlight. And you were tired, but you didn't want to go to sleep and lose any of it."

"The beacon lights flashed, red and green."

My spine tingled. Music-tingle, not cold-tingle. "The beacon was an ebony pyramid —" I murmured.

"That's nice," he said. "It sounds good the way you say it. You must like poetry."

I looked down at my shoes and nodded. "Do you?" I asked shyly.

He shook his head. "I'm physics, myself."

"There's nothing wrong with physics," I said staunchly. Actually I wasn't too sure what was included.

"Well, there's nothing wrong with poetry, either."

There didn't seem to be any more to say. I could see that he wasn't going to talk just so that we'd be talking. He was perfectly happy sitting.

He noticed that he was still holding my stone.

If he gave it back to me and we weren't talking, what would I do? I would have to go. Where? Desperately, I tried to think what would interest him.

"We have a sloop," I said. The words all tumbled out in a terrible rush. "Two suits of

Ratsey sails." I tried to be as physical as possible.

He looked at me steadily. "You'd be all right," he said, nodding. I felt that he was seeing me, not in the idiot dress, but in a sweatshirt and rolled jeans, with bare feet, trimming the sheet as we raced along to windward in a spanking, spray-slapping breeze.

"We have a spinnaker and a Genoa," I added urgently. Suddenly I was bursting to tell him about every beloved piece of gear. "The spinnaker has —"

"You'd be mad for Cuttyhunk," he interrupted, spilling over with words also. He leaned forward in his chair.

I knew that I should let him talk.

"See, the island is like a lagoon," he said. He made an open circle with his arms, the fingers of one hand still curled around the stone.

"In the center of the island is this big basin. *Looks* like a perfect harbor. To the lubbers, that is."

I could see the salt-grass and dune-encircled lagoon. I wiggled down in my chair and pulled part of the cover around my chilly shoulders.

"But here's the kicker," he said. His eyes lit up suddenly and began to laugh. I could tell there was a funny landlubber yarn coming. "See, at *low* tide only about a third of the basin is deep enough to take the keel boats. But at *high* tide it's all safe. There's about a six-foot differential."

He gave me back the stone while he talked. It was warm from his hand.

"So . . . by five o'clock in the evening," he continued, "the safe part of the basin is full. Of real sailors, who follow their charts."

I kicked off my slippers and curled my feet comfortably under my skirt. For a moment I thought I heard footsteps in the corridor, but they went away.

"Then about eight o'clock," he was saying, "comes the grand lubber procession, weaving down the channel, side-swiping every buoy —"

"Flying the cocktail flag?" I asked.

"Three sheets to the wind." He nodded. "So . . . Dad says to one Slobby Joe —"

"With a just too yachty cap?"

"So right. Dad says, 'I think we can make room for you alongside.' But Joe answers (he was really corked), 'Avast there, BUDDYROO. We're gonna park over there where there's LOSSA ROOM!' "

"Park!" I said. I covered my mouth with my hands. My face felt flushed and rosy.

"So Joe parks." He was talking fast now. "He drops anchor on the *high* tide. Around eight p.m. Then he and his frau drink a couple more pitchers of martinis and hit the sack."

"So the tide is low around two a.m.," I said, catching on. "You've got to be kidding!" I squealed, but I shut up. I didn't want to spoil his story.

"It's the middle of the night." He was enjoying the memory. "And they wake up to a sixty-degree list. Dad puts our big spot on them —"

"Oh, no!" I groaned. "It's too good!"

"There were eight boatloads of lubbers, all

of them hopping around in a foot and a half of muddy water —"

"I can see the lady lubbers," I gasped, "in their nightgowns . . . and prickly curlers —"

"One guy was yelling at this lady . . . and she was screaming at him —" he was having trouble getting it out, "— and she was actually scooping up handfuls of mud . . . and slinging it — " He had to stop.

I wiped my eyes.

"Did you . . . did you ever watch a motorboat lubber fill his wa-ter tank with gas?" I had trouble finding enough breath to tell it.

"It's not possible!" he said.

"He stuck the gas hose right into the water intake —" I listened because I heard footsteps again. But I had to finish. "He stood there and waited and waited and waited. And finally he said to Dad, 'Mister, I wonder if you could tell me . . . why this boat is taking . . . such a terrible lot of —' "

"*Jo*-sieeee?" I heard. It was Mother. "Josie, *dar*ling," she called, plaintively. It was her oh-my-poor-baby voice.

"Now that is a real *gas*ser!" said my friend. His eyebrows went up with pleasure at his own joke.

"You!" I said, looking at him sideway, smiling. Sometimes it comes to you, what to do.

Mother appeared around the corner. "Oh!" she said. "Ex-cuse *me!*" Her eyes got big and round. "I was looking all — I just thought —" She backed up. "It's time for the Last Dance." She was having her troubles. "— I didn't know —" Exit one confused parent.

"That was my mother," I said, standing up.

I felt a sudden chill. "I guess I'd better go." The cold tile was sending icy shivers up my legs. My feet groped their way into shoes. "I have an aunt —" I snapped my bag shut with clammy hands. "She thinks everyone has to be on the floor for the . . . Last Dance." My voice was weariness itself.

"I read you loud and clear," he said, standing up too. "I, also, have . . . obligations" — he looked at his watch — "which I see I have avoided for most of the evening. With great success."

We walked down the corridor, slowly, and came to the entrance to the dance floor. Aunt Anne and Priscilla were standing in front of the door. Peering here and there on tippytoes.

"My obligation can really dance," he said, "but she sure wasn't around when they were passing out brains." He was almost whispering. An idea was flickering in my head, but he went on. "Now," he said, and his eyes smiled at me, "what about you? Josie?"

I would have died sooner than have him know I didn't have a partner. I had to escape to the ladies' room and I tried to figure out what was the proper way to say it. Priscilla always said, "I have to go *fix* my *face*," but I —

Priscilla had turned around and noticed us. She was whispering to Aunt Anne. Aunt Anne turned around too.

The music started with a crash.

"I guess I'd better —" I started. I looked at him.

He was staring at Priscilla the way some people stare at a snake, with horror, but with fascination.

Aunt Anne looked at me and said something to Priscilla. Priscilla snickered. Aunt Anne gave her a little push in our direction.

I was sure.

"Henry Bassett?" I said, shyly.

"How did you know?" he asked. He looked from Priscilla to me.

I backed out onto the dance floor and switched my hair back and forth so that the fuzzy ends brushed my bare shoulders.

Priscilla was zeroing in on me, flanked by Aunt Anne.

"Hey! Henry!" I taunted. Putting my arms out to the sides and snapping my fingers to the music, I eased into my slow stomp, twisting my body as I turned.

"Like wow!" said Henry. He broke into a faster step and I followed.

"She's your cousin," I shouted, teasing him. "You'd better dance with her."

"Kid me not!" Henry answered. He grabbed my handbag and stuffed it into his pocket and we really cut loose.

I saw Priscilla's stunned face.

It was a wild band. Plenty of sax and rowdy drums. Each of my joints was a separate swinging swivel. I went 'way, 'way down and 'way back. My arms pumped like pistons.

Henry pulled me in close. The music throbbed and we spun around tight for a chorus of slow bars before he flung me out again. My feet were hardly touching the floor.

Aunt Anne was trying to get the crummy boy from her block to dance with Priscilla. But he wasn't exactly jumping at the opportunity.

Mother's face was a caution. Shocked and

pleased at the same time. As though she'd like to take me home right this instant and put me in a hot tub, but at the same time get out on the dance floor with me.

Aunt Anne was comforting Priscilla. They both looked as though they'd been caught in a disaster area.

Suddenly the crummy boy appeared and tried to cut in. "What-say —" he started.

"Buzz off!" I hollered.

Henry gave him a push in the chest so that he skidded across the floor and almost collided with the bass drum.

"Don't let it fade!" Henry yelled at the drummer, and the snares hammered up a new thunderstorm. It was all percussion and the drummer was way out. Most of the other couples had left the floor and were standing around watching us, clapping it up, stomping with the beat until the floorboards shook.

I saw Aunt Anne lead Priscilla into the ladies' room.

"Go, girl, go!" the drummer shouted as he whack-bam-whacked his cymbal with the wire whisk.

Too soon it was over. Mother rounded me up and I floated into the coat room, flapping my wings, with Henry right behind. I was on Cloud One Hundred and Eleven. I did a couple of pirouettes.

"Josephine!" snapped Aunt Anne.

I hadn't noticed them. Standing there, all buttoned up, beside the coat rack, I could have sworn they were a couple of coats on hangers. Then I saw that the coats had Grant Wood faces.

"Wasn't it nice of Henry to give the Last Dance to your poor cousin Josephine?" said Aunt Anne to Priscilla in what I believe is known as a stage whisper.

"He probably noticed that no one else danced with the poor thing all evening," hissed Priscilla.

"*He* didn't exactly give anyone else a chance," whispered Henry, winking at Mother and me. Then he added, a little louder, so that Priscilla heard for sure, "May I drive Josie home, ma'am?"

Mother cleared her throat. "In a couple of years," she said, with a sweet smile, but a no-nonsense voice. Even when Mother gets a bit off balance, she has a remarkably rapid recovery time.

It was rather small of her. After all, I'd be fifteen in January. Only two more months. But it didn't matter.

A mother can get in the way (and you need them to sometimes). You can get around them, though. I learn fast when I'm in the mood.

I wondered if she knew that Henry went away with my handbag still in his pocket. I didn't say a word to stop him. I thought he'd remember whose it was. Because of the stone.

3

Putting Away
Childish Things

After the Thanksgiving dance I was a different person. As different as night and day. Everybody said so. I was thoughtfulness and loving-kindness itself. I couldn't be nice enough to my family. I only wished there was some way to erase every memory of the intolerable way I used to be.

All day Saturday after the dance I helped Mother polish silver while I waited in the house for Henry to return my bag. I expected that when he came he would ask me to write and I decided that I would hesitate and then say yes.

Late Sunday afternoon I *had* to go out for a few minutes to take back a math book to a girl two blocks away. It was the worst day in my whole life. I left the house for only a minute. It was hard to understand how he didn't see me walking down the street. He drove up right after I left and returned the bag to Mother.

But if you felt that way about someone you could wait forever. Or at least you could wait until nine thirty p.m. on December twenty-eighth, the moment that the Christmas Get-Together was to start. It wasn't any time at all.

Every evening I brushed my hair hard for fifeen minutes and I washed it twice a week. Soon it shone like a newly husked chestnut and it waved smoothly at the ends.

I was in such a tearing hurry for Christmas to come that I surprised Mother by putting up all the Christmas decorations two weeks early, one afternoon when she was downtown.

Grammy bought me a new dress for Christmas and I tried so many different shades of lipstick with it that Dad said to Mother, "Josie must think we own stock in Woolworth's," and Mother frowned.

Christmas morning Aunt Anne and Uncle Jack and Priscilla came over. Aunt Anne gave me a pretty compact, green enamel with an inlaid rose, like a cameo. I said, "Thank you very much, Aunt Anne," and my eyes watched her finger the balsam to see if it was fresh and my ears heard her tell Mother where she could have done better, but the real me was at the dance already, only three days away, being whirled around the floor.

Then I had a blow. At Christmas dinner (it was Grammy's turn, but she decided at the last minute that she "wasn't up to it," so Mother had to do it) I overheard Aunt Anne tell Mother that Henry's family was taking him South for Christmas. It was "too tiresome" because she thought she had Henry all lined up "to squire Priscilla around" to all the "doings."

Bad as I felt, I couldn't help smiling behind my napkin. I was certain that Henry made his family take him South just to give Aunt Anne the slip.

It was a terrible disappointment not to be seeing him at Christmas, but, as I whispered to Mother when we got up from the table, "It doesn't really matter. They can't keep us apart forever. There's always the Spring Get-Together." And Mother answered, sourly, "Don't I know it!"

Actually, I had a whiz-bang time at the Christmas dance. Peter couldn't keep his eyes off me. He followed me everywhere and he cut in and cut in. After a while I had to say, "Oh, Peter, for heaven's *sakes!*"

Peter wanted my picture for Christmas in the worst way. I didn't care too much about giving Peter one, but I thought it might be useful to have some pictures taken in case . . . anyone else asked. I said, "It's just for a boy in my Latin class." Mother grumbled a lot, but she gave in. She handed out all the extra prints, but I knew I wouldn't have any difficulty with Grammy when I needed one back.

From the way Peter was acting I knew that something was sticking out all over me. I always tried out the New Me on Peter. If Peter liked my clothes and my new hairdo (I'd always say, "Hey, Peter. What do you think?"), I figured Henry would. Peter sat next to me in every class that we had together. He took me to several basketball games and once we went for a long walk with his dog, Spike. Peter was very useful.

If only there had never been an Old Me. Some things that person had done in the past made me actually blush. I was looking forward to my birthday because I figured being fifteen would wipe out the mistakes of being fourteen. The way Dad's mistakes got wiped out when his new driver's license came. He could forget about the old mistakes as if they never happened.

I was positive that I was through with my old self. I didn't think that anything or anyone could throw me off balance again.

I should have known myself better.

January sixteenth was my birthday. I stood at the kitchen sink that morning, humming a cheerful tune, happily thinking how I had never seen a colder, snowier, more miserable January in all my born days.

I scraped an eggy plate. (Paul never would eat the yellow part for me.)

Suddenly Dad announced, "Josie, Paul and I are going . . . uh . . . to the hardware store for some . . . er . . . um . . ."

Anyone could hear that he was making it up. But why?

"For some *hard*ware," said Paul. He giggled that bubbly way he does when he knows something he isn't supposed to tell.

"Yup, Paul," said Dad. "I guess that's right." And he started to chuckle up a storm.

I still didn't catch on. Of course, I remembered that it was my birthday. But I also knew that when Mother left for Aunt Anne's in such a hurry the night before, right after Dad's plane came in, she didn't have time to say a thing to him about my birthday. When Aunt

Anne's back "goes out," believe me it has priority.

Suddenly I got it. Paul and Dad were going to buy my birthday present. And they didn't know what I wanted.

"I'm going too," I announced. I wiped my hands on my skirt.

It isn't that I was the kind of kid that cared about Things. At fifteen you're over that. But what I wanted for my fifteenth birthday was something special. I had to have it. The way I sometimes have to have a certain book or record album; when what you get out of the thing is much more than what it costs. It's like starving for it.

I'd been putting off and putting off telling Mother what I needed because I didn't want to hear her say "No!" And she'd been trying to find out for weeks what it was. Probably so she could say, "There. Now I've got Josie's present off my list." (Not to knock Mother, but she can be pretty listy.)

So the afternoon before my birthday, the minute I walked in the door and stamped the slush off my feet, Mother said, "Josie, I don't mean to *pry* or anything like *that,* but since tomorrow is the Big Day, don't you think you'd better let me in on this birthday-present thing?"

"It's fish," I blurted, surprised into saying it. I dropped my books on the kitchen table.

"Fish?" said Mother, in a mixture of a question and an exclamation. She looked as though she'd had a sudden whiff of a bad one.

I knew it all along underneath. Mother never thought anything about fish in her whole life except to ask if the filet of sole was nice and fresh.

"Fish in a tank," I said. In my mind I could see the tank standing in the corner of my bedroom. A watery world of emerald greens. Illuminated. Schools of silver slivers; turn, flash, and turn —

"*Gold*-fish," said Paul.

I didn't even know that he was hanging around. His head was just about as high as the ironing board.

"Absolutely not goldfish," I said. "Goldfish are for babies. Tropical fish, for your information. And I have to pick them out myself. Mother, can I? Please?"

Mother's face got the look I expected. "They are awfully expensive, aren't they?" she asked gently. "Don't you need a lot of fancy equipment to keep them alive?"

We both knew the answer.

"Why don't you like *gold*-fish?" asked Paul. "They are so pretty and —"

"I'd need the tank, and a heater, and the filter. And a motor —"

I stopped. Right then I knew that never in a hundred years would Mother get me all that stuff. Even if we could afford it she wouldn't approve.

"And what else?"

"And the rocks. And the gravel. And this special little tank for the babies —" I could imagine the tiny babies swimming around.

"We haven't even come to the fish."

I shook my head. I could see we never would come to the fish. How old do you have to be so you don't have to cry? I could feel the tears coming and I hated them because I knew they would upset Mother.

"Things are tough all over," said Paul. He was trying the string of the ironing board cover in lots of irritating knots.

"You don't un-understand . . . how im-important —" I said.

"I almost care," said Paul, in his rudest voice.

"Shut up," I said.

"Now wait a minute," said Mother. (She looked the way I felt.) "If there's something that someone really wants around here, we can usually work it out." She was talking slowly. Thinking. "Say we get you the tank tomorrow . . . for your birthday —"

"Josie said, 'Shut up,' " said Paul, expecting sympathy.

He didn't get any.

"Hush," said Mother. "How much would the tank cost? About twenty dollars?"

I nodded. Mother handed me a tissue.

"You can earn money for some of the parts over the winter and spring. Baby sitting," she went on. "And you can ask for the rest of it for Christmas if you haven't been able to save up enough. It isn't forever."

Christmas! It was too forever. Christmas was just over.

It wasn't fair when people got between you and the things you wanted. It made you have to choose between People and Things. Like the night in September when I wanted to go down to the shore and Aunt Anne wanted me to play bridge. When you were grown up, it seemed, you were always supposed to choose people. I wondered if I would ever be grown up enough to automatically and naturally see things and people in the proper perspective. So that I wouldn't have to listen to any more "Josie, dear, you simply must learn to be more aware of other people's feelings." Big Choice!

"It isn't fair —" I started.

And the phone rang. It was Aunt Anne. The old back had popped a disc again and Mother had to run right off. I said to myself, "If you ask me Aunt Anne just likes to spend the weekend in bed every once in a while and get a lot of sympathy."

There wasn't time to tell Dad about my present. I knew Mother didn't have time. I figured he'd naturally forget my birthday, or wait until Mother got back from Aunt Anne's. So when he and Paul started to go through this vaudeville routine about the hardware store ("Yup, Paul, I guess that's right, boy; we're going to the *hard*ware store to buy some *hard*ware.") it was a minute before I caught on. And I couldn't think what to do about it except to say, "I'm going too."

Mother would ask why didn't I say, right then and there, "Look, Dad, I'll just bet you and Paul are going to get my birthday present. I think that's terrific, but actually I talked to Mother about something special that she said I could have. Do you mind terribly if I tell you what it is?"

It wasn't all that easy.

Mother might have remembered why it was that even if I lived to be a hundred years old I could never say a thing to Dad about any present except, "Thank you very much, Dad, for the lovely present. It's exactly what I wanted." She might have remembered that the Original People-vs-Thing Stink of All Time happened between me and Dad early in October when he brought me — But I was still trying hard not to think about that. All through October, all through November, December, January I had managed to keep it blotted out of my memory. It wasn't fair to hold it against me. After all, it had happened before I was a different person.

How long does it take for an embarrassing and humiliating experience to fade away? So that you lose the feeling that it is happening all over every time you are reminded of it? Maybe you have to endure the feeling, like penance, until you are sure you'll never let yourself get into the same situation again, or until you've, somehow, had the opportunity to make up for it.

That was why I thought the best thing would be if I went along to the (oh goody!) hardware store (in quotes) with Paul and Dad. My announcement really finished them both off. I thought they would flip. Paul had rolled off his chair and he was staggering toward the back door as if he had been shot in the back. Any kind of a secret completely did him in. Then, too, any time he could get Dad downtown without Mother, Dad would buy him the moon. (Me, too, but I was too *old* to take advantage.) I could imagine Paul easing Dad into traipsing around Woolworth's (with a side order of Liggett's). And with *such* an al-truistic reason for being there in the first place! Paul thought he had his morning made.

So when he saw his plans beginning to fizzle, he stood and gawked up at Dad. I wouldn't have been surprised if Paul had lain right down on the floor and started kicking any minute.

Then Dad pulled rank. His solution to everything those days.

"Josie, I think . . . uh . . . Mother would like you to finish the housework first."

Putting it on Mother was also popular.

"I'll do it later," I insisted.

"Let's not be difficult," said Dad.

I stared at him, remembering how he used to think the habit was cute.

"Josie, *please,* dear," said Dad, "let's not start that now." I had him unnerved. *"Be* a good girl. We won't be gone long."

"Josie's eyeballs are going to fall out," said Paul, tugging at Dad's sweater.

"Shut up!" I said, turning on him.

Dad slipped out the back door.

"Why don't you act your age, not your shoe size?" said Paul. He made a disgusting face and ran out and slammed the door.

I jerked the handle, but Paul was holding it outside. "You lose!" he said. I heard Dad start the car.

"Little brat!" I shouted. I kicked the door.

I heard the car door slam. Out the kitchen window I saw snow spurt up behind the tires and they were gone.

"SO WHAT!" I shouted, loud and rude, as if they were still there to hear. "WHO CARES!"

Dad's pipe was lying on its side next to his coffee cup. He hadn't time to finish his coffee. It looked stale brown, cold and lonesome.

"If they get me something grubby and I don't like it I'll have Mother exchange it," I said, out loud, but not so loud as before.

I knew that Dad would be feeling in his jacket pocket for the pipe. It wouldn't be there. He wouldn't say anything and he'd put his hand back on the wheel. But he'd miss it. I shivered with more than the cold.

"When Mother returns Dad's present, I'll use the money for the fish tank," I whispered. I was almost afraid of the sound of my voice.

I ran upstairs to my bedroom and it was better there. My room was so perfect! Mother and I did it over in October, as she had promised. We started as soon as we got back from the shore, although Mother did say, after I told her about the row with Aunt Anne, that she wasn't at all sure I deserved it. We painted the walls a pale apple green. I chucked out all my old baby stuff. (Paul grabbed it before it hit the floor.) Where the doll house had been, the fish tank was going.

I put the Chopin Preludes on the record player. (Since Thanksgiving nothing but Chopin would do.) And I sat down at my desk. The middle drawer was where I kept the catalogue and the drawings. I tried to keep it locked since Paul had a hack session in it one time, but it was hard to remember. If there is one thing he is crazy about, it is my belongings. The grass is always greener, Mother says.

I took out my pastels and the sketch that I was working on. The sketch had agate rocks (marbled red and white) piled up high on the left, to hide the filter. But you could see a necklace of silver bubbles rising behind the rocks. I loved the bubbles. I did them just right, with shading. On the right, to balance, feathery fronds fanned up and out. High toward the back, the sandy gravel rippled down in tiny dunes to the front, with no ornament, except perhaps my round white stone (when I could spare it from everyday duty). Suspended in one corner, a wee plastic tanklet, for the babies.

For what reason were the veined rocks, the fluffy branches, the silver circles from the filter? From the catalogue: A Pearl Danio? A Jewel Tetra? No. Two Siamese Fighting Fish, a red and a black, nose to nose in bug-eyed wonder.

I hooked my hair over my ears and began to draw. Lightly, with a pencil at first. Scale by scale.

Not enough light. I reached for the lamp.

Sometimes when you are waking up in the morning and you are warm and comfortable and happy in a good dream, you suddenly have the feeling that something is awfully wrong, but for a little bit you have to grope around to find out what it is.

I had that feeling in the kitchen when Dad and Paul said they were going to the hardware store and I had it even worse when I snapped on the lamp switch.

Then you remember the thing that is wrong and it's something that no one can fix, like your bird died, or you got an awful mark on an exam, or you were embarrassingly rude to a relative.

I remembered when I looked at the lamp.

The base was a shiny black kitty, sitting up

on its haunches. In its chubby paws it held the handle of a parasol. The parasol was the lampshade. Pink and frilly, with stiff lace and little bows . . .

. . . It had happened the October afternoon that Mother and I finished my room. I had kept it out of my mind since then. We had really been pushing to get the painting done. Mother wanted to finish while it was still warm enough to have the windows open, before we had to think about Thanksgiving. She didn't think the smell of paint would do a thing for the turkey.

We were both exhausted. I never saw a room in my whole life that looked so wonderful. We had put the rug down and the furniture was arranged a new way.

I didn't put one single thing back into my room that wasn't perfect. I said to Mother, "I'm really putting away childish things today, aren't I?"

She looked at me the way she does when she is going to say something and then decides not to. "Mmmm," she murmured.

I was fixing my books on the shelves, thinking what a good way this was to start the school year, when Dad called to say which train he was on. I heard Mother tell him, "It would be very nice, but it isn't really necessary," and then I changed the record.

It was getting dark outside. The maple tree at my window was a glorious red-gold mass against the evening sky. The leaves made a crisp sound as they fell, because it hadn't rained.

Mother came back into the room and said there would be time to put up the traverse rods and hang my curtains (crisp white, like the bedspread) because Dad would be a little late. I was tired and hungry, but I wanted to finish.

(Even when I didn't want to, when I got this close to it, I had to go on and go over the whole thing in my mind.)

We were just done with the curtains and Paul was getting fussy about dinner when I heard the front door slam and Dad came up the stairs. He was carrying a brown paper package.

"Oh, my!" he said. He looked around my room as if he was in a strange house, and then he looked at Mother. "Josie really —" and then his voice trailed off.

He held out the lumpy bundle to me. "A surprise for your new room," he said.

I took it from him.

Paul started to pick at the knot.

"I didn't know quite what —" said Dad, frowning. He reached out with his pocketknife and snapped the string.

The paper fell away and there it was. The horrible ugly cat lamp. For me. To put in my beautiful room.

"I thought . . . for your desk —" he said, watching my face.

If he had taken a can of screaming red-purple paint and splashed it all over everywhere it would have been about the same.

I sort of tried to hand it back to him. "I . . . I really was thinking more of a . . . glass lamp, Daddy," I said.

54

"Let's try it and see," said Mother, in her in-between-two-people voice. "And if it isn't —"

"It gives a good strong light," said Dad, pushing a cheerful voice. He plugged it in. "Look." The pink parasol shed its gaudy light, muddying the delicate apple green.

"Daddy, I don't want —" I started.

"Josie, your father has gone to a lot of trouble to bring you a present," said Mother. She was scowling at me over Dad's shoulder. He hadn't taken his hat off yet, even.

"You haven't seen the best part," said Dad, heartily. He reached behind the cat's head and flipped a switch. The cat's eyes glowed like great green marbles.

"Oh! Grand!" said Paul. He cooed, overcome with pleasure and snapped the switch on and off. "We can put it in the window on Halloween! When the kids come Trick or Treating!"

"Paul!" said Dad. "Let Josie do it. It's her lamp."

"I hate it!" I said. "Get it out of my room!" On and off. On and off.

"See?" said Dad. "Paul likes it."

"It's a lamp for a baby," I shouted. "Can't you see? I'm not a baby any more!"

Dad looked stunned. Shocked. Hurt.

"Shameful child!" said Mother.

"If Josie doesn't like it," said Dad, appealing to Mother, "I can —"

"Let me deal with this," said Mother. She patted his arm and eased him and Paul out of the room and shut the door softly with her back so that she was facing me.

The cool October breeze blew the curtain corners gently. I sat down on the edge of my bed. I almost couldn't stand up any more.

Mother was so mad she couldn't speak. When she did, it came out quieter than I expected.

"Since you claim to be so grown up, young lady," she said in a low voice that was tight and choked, "I think you are old enough to consider which is more important. The aesthetics of a lamp? Or an individual's feelings?"

She started to open the door and then turned on me again. "What do you think it really means?" she said. "To put away childish things?" She slammed out.

Mother was mad. But I wasn't too bothered. Mad is better than hurt. Mad gets over with.

Sometimes when a dog kills a chicken, they hang one around its neck.

Or in *The Ancient Mariner* they hung the albatross around his neck. ". . . instead of the cross, the albatross —"

The lamp was my albatross.

Most unpleasant experiences you can forget about. But almost four months have passed since that autumn evening and still I felt it there in my mind as an ugly thing. Even in January it was building up inside until I knew I couldn't feel better unless I went through the whole miserable business in my mind again. It almost fascinated me, in a horrible sort of way. And I told it to myself all over again.

I could see my daddy at the end of a grueling day's work. He was trudging toward the distant, dimly lit line of stores, his pipe clenched between his chattering teeth. Night had fallen and the winter air was chill. Tired and hungry, shivering in his threadbare overcoat, mile after mile he tramped bravely onward, his patient face lined with care. At long last he espied the lamp in the window. He clasped his hands! Oh joy! How his weary eyes lit up at the thought of pleasing his little girl. His precious baby, who was all the world to him. He took the last bill from his worn wallet. Burdened, he labored homeward. With trembling hands he offered her his hard-won gift. And she —

"Oh, Daddy!" I sobbed. Through familiar tears I saw the cat. I reached around and flicked the switch. "Cat," I said, searching the depths of its glassy eyes. "Help me."

So hard I looked, that all I saw was a green blurry glow. Like the watery green of a fish tank.

"*You* think I should wait till Christmas," I said to the cat, "if I can't earn the money. I suppose it won't be forever," I said, sniffling. "It's only ele-ven months."

A good feeling was starting inside exactly where the bad one had been. Lots of times that's how you know when you've decided something right.

"All right," I said, "I'll ask for my fish for Christmas, if I haven't earned them by then. And I absolutely promise you, Cat," I said, solemnly, "that no matter what Dad brings me today or at any other time in my whole life, I will never ask Mother to exchange it, and I will say 'thank you' as though I mean it."

The cat looked steadfastly back.

"You win, Cat," I sighed. "I will mean 'thank you.' Whatever he brings me. I vow it. Thank you for the trouble . . . and . . . the love."

I tidied up my pastels and my catalogue. The Siamese Fighting Fish were all smeary with tears.

"It would be a lot easier if I didn't want the fish so much," I said. My voice was shaking.

"Stop being so sorry for yourself," I said, louder. That sounded better.

I looked at myself in the mirror. It was a terrible sight. I combed my hair down straight, but I was still no prize. Then I remembered the green enamel compact that Aunt Anne had given me for Christmas. I'd had it for a month, but I'd never opened it. I found it in my top bureau drawer and broke the paper with my fingernail and put some powder on my nose and under my eyes. It hid the red spots. I looked better.

I could see why they said I looked like Grammy, the way she used to look when her hair was thick and burnished chestnut.

Of course she didn't have bangs. I pushed mine back. My eyes were big and far apart, like Grammy's. Grammy always said we got greater depth of vision than other people from them. One time I heard Aunt Anne tell Mother that I had "fine" eyes, but the way she said it made it sound as though the rest of my face was too bizarre for words.

I was happy to look like Grammy. Dad told me once that Grandfather considered Grammy a great beauty and that he spoiled her rotten. I wondered if anyone would ever spoil me rotten for that reason.

I smiled at my reflection. "Hello, there, Different Person," I said.

Thoughtfulness and loving-kindness flooded back through me. With all the happiness that had been mine since Thanksgiving, how could I be so childish as to fuss at my father about a tankful of fish?

There were a million ways to get my fish. It was just a question of looking at the situation properly. Lots of times Grammy helped when I needed something, though it made Mother cross. Then, too, I could buy second-hand equipment with the money that Mother was willing to spend on the tank. And I was making a mint baby sitting.

I put the powder away and slammed the papers back in my drawer. "Until Christmas, even, if necessary," I said.

I whistled through Paul's room and did the dishes and mixed the tuna fish and scraped the carrots for lunch. I was just done when I heard the car tires scrunching on the crusty snow.

Out the kitchen window I could see that Dad and Paul were each carrying a large package. It was difficult to see how Dad could ever buy me a present again. Unless he was absolutely sure what I wanted. Maybe he wasn't as upset about the lamp as I was, but still it must have been hard for him. For a minute I wanted to run back up to my room, but I stood firm, with my arms crossed, and waited.

Paul burst in first. His face was like the sun, he was so happy.

"Bet you thought we forgotted!" he said. He put his package on the table. It was largish, and square.

Dad came in behind and set his bundle next to Paul's. It was about the same size, only round. Dad was smiling to himself, holding it in the way you do when you don't want anyone to know you are feeling silly with pleasure.

"Mine first," said Paul.

I sat down on the chair and slid the string off Paul's package. I tried to stay sort of numb, to keep from showing how disappointed I felt, by chanting to myself, like a charm, "I'll earn some of the money. Grammy will help me. I'll ask for the rest for Christmas."

I got Paul's present open and it was an enormous chartreuse handbag, of fake suede, with big plastic handles. It was really too much. On one side was a pink and fuschia sequined poodle with a glowing rhinestone eye. It was enough to make you want to —

"Paul, I never saw anything like it!" I said.

"You can keep your junk in it," said Paul. "It costed one-forty-nine." He pointed to a tag which showed three reductions.

"I'm mad for it," I said. "I had to have it."

"See the eye?" he crooned.

How could I miss it? It was the most vulgar eye in Westchester County.

"I asked the lady how many carrots there were in it," he went on. "You know it's important for eyes to have lots of carrots."

I tried not to laugh. "Paul. It's the craziest, wickedest eye in town," I said. "How did you know exactly what I wanted. I mean *the* actual thing?"

He didn't know which way to look, with pride and with pleasure. He sat on his hands and squirmed. I loved him.

"There's a surprise from Mother and me, too," said Dad, still all smiles.

I had forgotten.

He pushed the round bundle toward me.

I said, "Thank you very much, Dad." I picked at the bristly string with stiff fingers. My hands were so cold they weren't working right.

Dad whipped out his pocketknife and snapped the cord. The brown paper fell off.

It was a goldfish bowl. Plain. Squat. Round. Of thick grayish glass.

Paul grabbed it. "Mother said she was gonna get you fish. Remember? So I told Daddy you had a passion for fish."

He picked a brown paper package out of the bottom of the bowl. "Look," he said. "Lookit the sweet little stones."

He emptied the bag and the artificially bright chips clattered into the dusty bowl. Paul scooped up the gaudy pebbles and let them rattle back into the glass, his eyes like a story-book King Midas.

"Paul!" said Dad. "Let Josie do it!" He pulled a white cardboard container from his pocket. "And here are your fish, love," he said.

My hands couldn't help shaking as I reached for the carton. I knew it before I looked in. Two ordinary goldfish swam in silly circles.

Dad and Paul waited for me to be pleased.

I watched the fish dart back and forth within their white confines, looking for a way out.

Dad was waiting expectantly, his unlit pipe in his hand.

Wonderfully, I was able to say, with a steady voice, "Daddy, they are lovely."

There was no hope at all. I couldn't earn fish, or work through Grammy. I couldn't even ask for fish for Christmas. Because now I *had* fish.

"You couldn't possibly have gotten anything nicer for me." (No fish. Ever.) "Really, Dad. It was *just* what I wanted." (He bought them for me because that was what he thought.)

I carried the bowl over to the sink to fill it. For real fish you had to let the water stand for three days.

"I'm glad they're the right kind," said Dad. He stuffed some tobacco into his pipe. "I had no idea there were so many different kinds of fish. Beautiful ones. Like blowing tinsel —"

"Daddy?" said Paul.

"— or bits of rainbows," Dad went on. "Of course, that kind needs a heater and filter —"

"Josie knows," said Paul impatiently. "She has that cat-alogue about them. Daddy. You forgotted the best part!" He reached into Dad's coat pocket and pulled out a rubber man in a diving suit.

"Out of the way," he squeaked, elbowing me aside at the sink. "Putt, putt, clockety. Pssst. Pssst," said Paul. "All hands to the winch." He waved the diver in the air.

"Josie?" said Dad.

"All clear below?" said Paul. "Lifelines clear?" I stood back. "Stand by to dive. DIVE

DIVE . . . ZOOM . . . SPLAT." He lowered the diver into the bowl with a plop. Up and down. Up and down. "He's got the bends!" shrieked Paul. "Isn't it WILD!"

But Dad was looking at me, not Paul. "Josie," he said slowly. "You wanted tropical fish." He shook out the match he had lit without putting it to his pipe.

"That's the word," said Paul, working the diver vigorously. "Tropical." Splash. "Josie said, '*Ab*-solutely not *gold*-fish. Goldfish are for babeee —"

I put my hand over his mouth. "The child is raving," I said.

Paul started to bite, so I had to let go. He dashed for the stairs. "You'll see," he said, scampering up.

"Josie," said Dad. "Is that what you wanted? Tropical fish?" The smiles were all gone.

I studied a sprung stitch on one toe of my loafer. The aesthetics of a fish tank? Or Daddy's feelings?

"Daddy, the goldfish are lovely. I mean that I adore them. And I really want to thank you —"

Overhead there was a splintering, shattering crash. We both looked up at the ceiling (it was my room above) then at each other.

"Paul?" called Dad. "All right?"

We heard small sobs and dragging footsteps. Paul came down the stairs and stood in the doorway, holding the fish catalogue. "I b-broke Josie's l-lamp," he blubbered.

"All right, Paul," said Dad. "All right, now, boy," he soothed. "Josie never did like that lamp, anyway."

"Oh, yes I did, Dad," I said, quickly.

He lit his pipe and looked at me over the top, in his droll way.

I started to giggle. "I was absolutely cra-zy about it," I said. "I don't see how I can *live* without it."

"You lie like a rug," said Dad. He took the catalogue from Paul, who was developing a cunning expression that I was all too familiar with. "Josie," said Dad, "give the goldfish to Paul."

Puffs of smoke surrounded his head.

"Whaaat?" I said.

Paul grinned. He could read Daddy like a book.

"Come on," said Dad. "We'll go get the tank and the filter. You can choose." He held out his hand. "And the motor and the gravel."

Paul rubbed his mouth. He glared at me. "Mother said she could only have —"

"Catch!" I said, throwing the container of goldfish to him.

He fielded his hush money deftly and checked to see that both fish were inside. He put them on the sink beside the bowl and the diver, and looked at me speculatively.

I didn't feel at all sure of him. "What else?" I asked, in a low voice.

"Can I have the eyes too?" he whispered.

"Eyes?"

"The cat," he said. "Those mean green eyes."

"That's blackmail," I said. I pretended to consider hard, tapped one foot, looked around the room, up at the ceiling.

"Please?" he pleaded. I had him worried.

"I guess . . . yes."

"Coming, kids?" said Dad. "All set?" He was riffling through the catalogue, enveloped in clouds of delicious-smelling smoke. "How about these Neon Tetras?" he asked, pointing to the colored illustration with his pipe stem.

"Siamese Fighting Fish?" I suggested. "A red and a black?"

"Kissing Gouramis?"

"And a special little tank for the babies —?"

Persons and Things — I can honestly say I never had a better birthday!

4

It Is Better to
Have Loved

I thought the Spring Get-Together would never come. From Christmas to my birthday wasn't bad. The fish tank helped. Dad spent several Saturdays working out mechanical problems with me. But once these were solved there was nothing to do except sit and look at the fish and wait.

It was a long four months. December, January, February, March. Usually I can make time fly by reading fiction. When I read a book, I *am* the person: Juliet, Heathcliff's Cathy, and even Holden Caulfield's Jane. But reading wasn't working any more. My eyes went over the pages, but I'd be thinking about myself. It was much more thrilling to be Josie.

The first two weeks of March dragged out interminably. When *the* week finally came I was so excited that I couldn't eat, and Mother said, "If you don't relax and get some sleep

you're going to look like an old hag, and *you
wouldn't want that, would you?*"

When the doorbell rang downstairs, I was
at the mirror finishing the last touch of lipstick. In my new rose-colored dress (Grammy
again) against the pale apple-green back-
ground, I was an absolute vision. I hugged
my sensational self.

"That must be Aunt Anne," said Mother.
Her reflection wore its most worried look.

What a relief! I was frantic to get out before
Mother had a chance to bring up a certain
subject.

I could hear Dad in the front hall, opening
the door. "All alone, Anne?" he boomed.

"Priscilla is getting there on her own," said
Aunt Anne.

So. That meant a boy was going to drive
Priscilla to the Spring Get-Together. For Priscilla that was about like graduating from college magna cum laude.

"I'm surprised to see you home tonight,"
Aunt Anne was saying to Dad.

"Now, Anne," said Dad. "Don't give me
that. You know perfectly well that if I'm out of
town I always catch a plane that gets me home
in time for dinner on Friday."

"Oh, I've known times —" she started.

"Well, not very many," he said. "And when
I do get held up, I always call."

It always made him mad when Aunt Anne
insinuated that he didn't spend enough time
with his family because he had to travel. He
had every reason to be annoyed with her. He
was everlastingly considerate of us when he

had to be away. He never gave us a moment's worry.

I missed the rest of the juicy family squabble because Mother interrupted.

"You'll be going over alone with Anne," said Mother. She kept opening my bag and nervously checking its contents and clicking it shut again.

"Not quite," I said. "The Creep will be with us. You know *what?*" I snapped out, spinning around to face her.

Mother jumped. She sure was jumpy. "What?" she asked, in a startled voice.

"There's a rumor going around that he was *born* in the back seat of Aunt Anne's car." I was bubbling over with fun and games. Also I hoped to divert Mother's attention and escape before she got around to running the same old tape through again.

"Josie, you stop that," said Mother. "You know what I mean." She reached into my coat pocket and pulled out a folded hankie and put it back for the fourteen-hundredth time.

"I'm ready to *go*, Mother," I said. I could have stamped my foot with impatience, but that would have started a big scene and delayed things further.

"You aren't going to give Anne any trouble, are you?" said Mother, more like a threat than a question.

It was true that Aunt Anne and I weren't famous for getting along, but I also recognized Mother's skillful use of delaying tactics. I wanted to say, "Aunt Anne and I aren't going to get along any better ten minutes from now," but I held my tongue and my breath and looked down at the floor.

Mother jittered around with my coat. "And about Henry —" she said.

My face got beet red. I could feel the blush spread to my ears and my neck and even down my bare shoulders. I hung my head and pretended to fumble through the top bureau drawer for my white gloves.

"They're on the bed," said Mother. "All I want to say is that I think you have been attaching a *great* deal too much importance —"

"I don't want to hear any more ab-out it, Mother," I said. I snatched my coat and swirled it around my shoulders. "He probably won't even be there," I said. (But I knew he would. I had asked Aunt Anne if I could see the list of acceptances "to find out if a girl from school was coming.")

"I just wish I'd been asked to chaperone this dance instead of the Thanksgiving one," said Mother, not fooled a bit. (She had probably asked to see the list too.) She reached for my bag again.

I got to it first. "At fifteen I hardly need a baby sitter," I said, haughtily.

"Well, don't say I didn't tell you —" Mother started.

"Really, Mother, I can take care of myself," I said, grabbing my gloves.

I am delighted she isn't coming, I thought. And I don't care if she knows it. I swished down the stairs, conscious of the pleasing rustle of my satin petticoats.

"Kitten!" said Dad. "You look lovely!"

(He'd been calling me Kitten since my birthday. I pretended to mind, but I didn't really.) He kissed me carefully, so as not to muss me. "Doesn't she look lovely, Anne?" he asked.

"She surely does," said Aunt Anne, looking me over sharply.

Driving over with Aunt Anne wasn't so bad. The boy sat in the back seat and I sat up front. It was beginning to be warm and a little like spring outside. Under the street lights at the intersections I could see that the forsythia was going to burst open soon to make yellow patches under the yellow lights. I drew in a deep, sweet breath. I hoped that Aunt Anne wasn't feeling picky, that she'd leave me alone to drift into my private dream world uninterrupted.

As I got older I found that I was getting along better with Aunt Anne. Especially when Priscilla wasn't around to get her kicks out of pitting us against each other.

Naturally, Aunt Anne didn't understand me. But I was willing to keep the lid on as long as she didn't try to get involved in my affairs or hand out any stage directions. I thought she'd learned that lesson pretty thoroughly the night at the shore. She had been unexpectedly kind after I apologized. We had both learned a lesson.

I looked at her profile in the intermittent light of the oncoming headlights. Her nose was sharp, like Dad's and Grammy's. I usually thought of her in terms of her nose: sharp and pokey. But in the car, softened by the shadows, her face looked faded, wrinkled, soft, and tired. Getting Miss Sixteen, the Teen-Age Queen, ready for a party must have been quite a workout.

"Josie, I said to your father as you were coming down the stairs, 'How that child has blossomed in a few short months!'"

Blossomed! If she only knew!

I looked out the window and went over it again. Every single cherished moment, memorized like a poem.

I had honestly been beginning to think that I was so peculiar and unattractive that no one would ever look at me that way. Ever!

Then came that unforgettable moment when we first laid eyes on each other. We knew at once that it was what we had been waiting for all our whole long lives.

Ever since that fatal night, for four whole months, every second he had walked softly by my side. I had traversed that eternity of days wrapped in an invisible luminous cocoon, with a shaft of light shining on me alone.

The minute I got home from the Thanksgiving dance I looked at my dreadful self in the mirror. What a woeful sight! I said to myself, "There are going to be some changes made!"

I only told a few of my friends. One of them asked why didn't he write? And did I get a Valentine?

They didn't understand. Prep school was a tough grind for a senior. Anyway, I said, maybe he didn't know where I lived.

We were so much the same. He loved sailing and poetry, the way I did. I never dreamed that in this whole wide world there was another mortal being so much like me.

"— Josie?"

"What, Aunt Anne?" I said.

"I said I'm in love with your dress."

I went shopping with Grammy the first day of spring vacation (I was in despair for some new clothes) and everything I put on made me think only, How would Henry like it?

". . . I said, it really brings you out, dear."

"Thank you, Aunt Anne."

I chose it for him. The color was called Wild Rose. The waist was tight and the skirt was full. It had frills up top (which helped no end) and just straps. Whee! Was I a Bomb!

When I got the dress home Mother said, "Well, Josie. I don't know. It isn't quite what you usually wear. I don't think I can trust you and Grammy —"

But I said, "Mother, I'm fifteen now." I talked her into it. I had planned to bring up the subject of Wild Rose nail polish, but she did so much muttering and grumbling and disapproving of what she called, quote, the whole situation, that I decided I'd better leave well enough alone.

Mother didn't understand.

Less than half an hour to go! Out of everyone in the whole room Henry would choose me. If I were to die that moment, I'd die happy. It would be a dream, a fantasy, a fairy paradise. And when Henry begged to drive me home (Mother wasn't chaperoning the spring dance, chuckle chuckle) Aunt Anne would be a push.

She was always highly in favor of what she called "affairs of the heart."

Seeing Henry at long last would be like seeing the golden sunrise —

"— Josie."

"I'm sorry, Aunt Anne. I didn't hear what you said."

"Child, you haven't heard a thing I've said to you for the last quarter hour."

"I'm really sorry," I said.

"I was saying we haven't done very well by Henry Bassett. We were to have him for a weekend in February, but all Uncle Jack managed was lunch with him in town."

It was weird — as if she followed my thoughts. I was glad it was dark.

"Remember him?"

I had to answer.

"Yes, Aunt Anne." I tried to say it primly, but it came out a little squeak.

She glanced quickly at me and then back at the road. For an awful moment I was afraid that Mother had said something. But Mother never confides in Aunt Anne. They aren't that close. Thank heavens! The chauffeur-passenger relationship was fine by me, but Aunt Anne didn't need to think that she was a mother-figure.

I leaned my head against the car window and thought of Byron's words: "They name thee before me, who knew thee so well." It was so beautiful, it gave me chills. Of course, the rest of the verse didn't fit: "Long, long shall I rue thee, too deeply to tell."

"I suppose he's very much in demand. He

is attractive," Aunt Anne chattered on. "I've heard through the family grapevine that he has a rather special girl." Her gold bangles jingled as she turned the wheel.

I hugged myself. If Mother heard *that* she wouldn't be quite so smart. It was all over town about Henry and me! The mother was always the last to know.

If only she knew, I thought, that the "special girl" was sitting right beside her. I was afraid I'd laugh out loud, so I closed my mouth tight for the rest of the ride.

The boy who rode over with us asked me to dance right off, almost before the music started. I didn't care. I'd dance with anyone while I was waiting. Three or four stags cut in on me and after that I chatted with one of the hostesses who was the mother of a friend of mine. I told her the decorations were just superb. I thought it was nice for her to feel that her efforts were appreciated. Of course, as soon as Peter came he monopolized me.

Aunt Anne kept nodding and smiling. Other than that she did a commendable job of minding her own business.

While I danced with Peter I planned, for the hundred and fiftieth time, how it would be when Henry walked into the room. Across the vast expanse of dance floor our eyes would meet. Unspoken words would fly between us. All the lonely yesterdays would melt as snow beneath the summer sun. In a rose-gold glow, a haze of happiness, I would behold him crossing the room. Gently he would take my hand from Peter's.

"Thank you, Peter," I whispered.

"What?" said Peter, bending his head down to hear over the din of the cha cha music.

"N-nothing," I murmured, startled.

Henry would waltz me away. "My Own," he would whisper. "My Very —"

"There's that guy you danced with at Thanksgiving," said Peter harshly.

I gasped.

The back of Henry's head was only a few feet from mine.

"Henry!" I cried, impulsively holding out my hands.

He turned and I saw beside him a blonde girl. Old, at least seventeen. Wearing a strapless, flesh-colored, sequined sheath.

He looked at me as though he was trying to figure out if I was the person who said his name.

They were holding hands even though they weren't dancing. Her hair was gluey with hair spray. They both looked at me politely. Waiting for me to explain who I was and what I wanted.

Her face became a pink-gray blur, with blue-green eyes. I almost couldn't stand up.

"Excuse me," I said. "I must have . . . made . . . a mistake."

They smiled at each other, the same private smile. He slid his arm around her waist and they walked away, whispering.

Somehow I got to the coat room. There wasn't anyone inside. I went to one corner and leaned against the wall, hanging my head. I couldn't cry or anything. I didn't know what to do next. Time went too slowly. "Oh, Mother, Mother," I whispered over and over. I wished

I'd pass out and crumple up on the floor. Then I wouldn't have to know what happened any more.

I heard the coat-room door open.

"*Jo*-sie?" called a familiar voice.

It was Aunt Anne. There was no escape.

I stood up straight with my back to the wall, both palms flat against it. Like facing a firing squad.

"Child!" she said, when she saw my face. "What's happened?"

She'll be glad, I thought. The joke's on Josie.

"I saw you talking to Henry Bassett and then I saw you run —"

Since her precious Priscilla couldn't have him she'd be de-lighted that I —

"Did Henry say something to upset you?" She looked at me sharply.

I thought, I'll die sooner than tell you. I drew in a deep gulp of air and tried to keep the room from spinning.

"Oh, Josie, dear," she said. "I feel so re-spons-ible!"

Her face puckered up as though she was going to burst into tears.

So I did.

She put her arm around my shoulder and I cried harder.

"I've made such a f-fool of-f my-s-self," I sobbed.

Mother would have said — well, in the first place she would have said, "Josie, I hate to tell you this, but I told you so." Then she would have carried on with, "All right now, young lady, there's no use crying over spilt milk; let's not fuss anymore; once bitten, twice shy, so we'll hope some good comes out of all this; let's pull yourself together now; we'd better get you right home now and into a hot tub; oh, dear, I told you so." And she would have disapproved thoroughly of the whole proceedings as though I'd disappointed her by being so unsensible. And she certainly couldn't have restrained herself from sprinkling that hateful word "infatuation" liberally over the whole brew.

Aunt Anne just kept me company for a while. She didn't disapprove at all. It was as though she understood everything that had happened to me since I danced the last dance with Henry the night after Thanksgiving many long months before.

So I told her all about it. Every single moment. Every wretched thought.

I began to feel a little better. If my situation was real to Aunt Anne (and it never was to Mother) then it was as if *something* had happened, even if it didn't turn out the way I dreamed.

Aunt Anne opened her bag when she saw that I was perking up; and she took out a compact like the one she had given me for Christmas.

"You know what I always say," said Aunt Anne, opening the box. "I always say —" she dabbed at my tear-stained cheeks, "— close your eyes — 'it's better to have loved and lost' —" the puff was soft on my swollen lids, "— 'then never to have loved' —"

"But he didn't," I said. "It was all a horrible mis-misunderstanding." I was ready to start crying all over again.

"Now, now," said Aunt Anne. "You didn't really lose." She turned me around facing the mirror. "Look at yourself."

I was pretty. Almost even something more.

"Six months ago I used to say to Priscilla —"

I didn't want to hear what she used to say to Priscilla.

"But Aunt Anne —"

"The point is *you* loved, dear child." She was studying my face, but I wasn't embarrassed.

"It changed you. We've all noticed. Can't you see it made a difference?"

It had. It was as if a lot of good stuff that was only inside me before had come out where people could see it. Even if I'd made a mistake, even if Henry hadn't recognized me, the last four months couldn't be erased. I couldn't snap back, like a rubber band, to exactly the way I was before it happened. It was true that I was a different person.

Aunt Anne understood, Mother didn't.

She clicked her bag shut. "Ready?" she asked.

"Oh, no!" I said, backing up against the wall again. "You can't make me go back out there. You aren't my —"

"That nice boy that's been so attentive all evening," she continued, in a calm voice, as though I hadn't spoken.

She meant Peter.

"He must be wondering what happened to you."

"I can't ever dance again," I said, facing her.

She was holding the door open for me, "Brave child," she whispered.

So I went out.

Henry and his — girl, if you wanted to call her that — were standing between me and the dance floor. I balked, but I felt Aunt Anne's warm arm at my elbow, so I went on with my nose in the air. As I passed him I switched my hair back and forth so that the smoothly waved ends brushed my bare shoulders. I could tell that he was trying to remember where he had seen me, but I wouldn't have looked at him if I'd been drowning in boiling tar.

I could be honest with myself; Mother was right. Sure Henry talked to me on the porch. He was bored to extinction. He'd have talked to a dog.

He never liked poetry. He was going to be a physicist. Probably he'd never even heard of Shakespeare.

Sure he danced the last dance with me. It was me or Priscilla. Some choice.

When he found, the next day, that he had my bag in his pocket — when you were eighteen and such a terrifically bright senior at such a sophisticated, brainy boarding school, you knew the way to deal with little fifteen-year-old girls who were . . . infatuated with you — you waited until you were sure they were out of the house and then you returned the bag to their mother.

A playback of Mother's tape. She was right. He didn't give me a particle of encouragement. I couldn't even hate him.

But what happened next?

"Where did you go?" asked Peter. He was standing beside me. "You missed refreshments," he said, one eyebrow up in the air, a mock-accusing expression.

I thought about how patient he was when he helped me with the hard parts of the Ovid.

But I still felt shaky and disoriented. Dancing was unthinkable.

"All set?" asked Aunt Anne. I knew she'd stand beside me like a bulldog as long as I needed her.

Mother would think that Aunt Anne's sympathy was sentimental nonsense. (Mother is the hot-tub type.) Maybe so. But Aunt Anne had helped me to keep my dignity. Mother was right, but right wasn't everything.

There might be different ways of looking at events. Mother could use her way when she was in a mess. But this was *my* mess and I was entitled to look at it *my* way.

Pride was the one thing I had left. I began to see that with a little effort on my part and a little cooperation from Aunt Anne, there was no reason to lose it.

"I'll be all set —" I said to Aunt Anne, "— as soon as you *promise not to tell Mother!*"

Mother was right, but she didn't have to know. I could pass up the "I told you so."

Aunt Anne looked startled at my tone.

Peter was evidence that something had happened to me. Aunt Anne had told me what it was. Who needed Mother?

"Come on, Jo," said Peter, taking my hand because the orchestra players were going back to their seats.

"Promise?" I whispered to Aunt Anne.

She nodded, and for a moment I thought she looked just the least bit pleased.

I had the biggest lump of unshed tears in my chest that I had ever had in my whole life, as I took my place beside Peter and answered his familiar reassuring smile.

But I could make them wait. "Some band!" I said to Peter.

And I would handle them alone.

5

The Most Terrible
Evening

I was numb inside. I was desolate. All
through vacation week, all Good Friday, I
moved around like a robot. I spent most of
the weekend in my room. My heart was made
of stone. I vowed never to be touched by anyone ever again. I put away Byron and got out
A. E. Housman. Never again would I give my
heart away.

I reveled in tales of unrequited love. It always helps to read about other people who
have the same experience. Like if someone
dies, you want to read stories about death. It
makes you feel less alone.

I tried to act absolutely natural, but Mother
and Dad worried about me. Mother did her
best to find out if anything had happened at
the dance; but all Aunt Anne (God bless
her!) would tell was that Peter had been very
attentive and that I had hardly been off the
floor all evening.

Several times, after that conversation, I

noticed Mother looking at me in a new way, with a sort of grudging respect, as though she had decided I was a separate, different individual that she was just getting to know.

To keep them from picking at me, I went through the motions. One of the motions was Peter. It was hard to say no to Peter. If Peter said, "Can you go to the basketball game Friday?" and I said, "No," he'd say, "How come?" It was less wearing to say yes in the first place. So, numb as I was I went where Peter asked me to go.

On the first Friday in April, thirteen days after the Spring Get-Together (I was still dating everything from that awful moment when my world crumbled) Peter called at seven o'clock to say that the basketball game had been canceled on account of bad weather.

"It must be pretty bad," I said.

"I heard over the radio that the Hutchinson River has flooded the parkway," he said. "It's coming down in torrents. We'll plan on next week." He hung up.

"Oh, dear. He's asked me for next week already," I groaned, looking out the living-room window. The storm was worse than it had been when I walked home from school. Wind hurled sheets of rain against the glass.

Since I couldn't go to the basketball game (that I'd been complaining all week I didn't want to go to) I felt, perversely, crosser. Not caring about anything gave me an ugly, sour, cramped feeling. My stomach growled along with the rest of me and I realized that I was quite desperately hungry.

Mother is one of those I-like-to-serve-promptly-at-seven people. An otherwise-we-have-no-evening type. So naturally by seven o'clock she has us all drooling on schedule, like Pavlov's dogs. But, lo and behold, it was seven fifteen already. She hadn't even called "Dinner!"

I went into the kitchen. How shocking! Almost seven twenty and my milk wasn't poured!

Paul was sitting at the table in his red pajamas, cuddling something black in his lap.

"Where's dinner?" I asked. I was in no mood to be trifled with.

Mother mumbled a few words that I didn't catch. She seemed touchy. Oh, no, I thought. What a terrible evening this is going to be!

"Where's Dad?" I asked. If Mother was grouchy it always helped to have Dad around.

Outside, a loose shutter banged and sleet hit the panes in bunches. The wind was ripping blossoms off the cherry trees and they stuck, wetly, against the glass.

"We'll give him a few more minutes," said Mother. She was fiddling around with a salad that already looked sensational.

"In a few more minutes I'll be a malnutrition case," I muttered. "How is he getting back from Providence?"

"The company he's working with this week has a company plane," said Mother. "He said they'd be landing around five thirty."

"I thought he didn't like to fly on company planes."

"He doesn't, but sometimes it's unavoidable."

The kitchen clock said seven thirty. "He should be home by now," I told Mother.

"The weather isn't too good," said Mother. "I expect —"

The phone rang and Paul jumped up to answer it, but Mother pushed him aside.

"I never get to answer it," said Paul, sitting down again. I saw that he was holding a big black water turtle.

"It'll be Daddy," I said. "Where'd you get the turtle?"

"School," said Paul. "His name is Hawaiian Eye. He's the First Grade Turtle. It's my weekend to have him visit."

Hawaiian Eye stuck out his rubbery neck full length, revealing glamorous yellow stripings.

"What a dear!" I said, sarcastically. A sudden hunger pang made me wince. When I visited Grammy, she let me eat any old time I wanted to. And every time I went she had a special coconut cake with lemon filling that she bought for me at this special bakery. But weekends with Grammy had been rationed lately. Mother complained to Dad that she was spoiling me rotten.

I listened to Mother's conversation. It wasn't Daddy.

"He's not home yet, Anne," Mother was saying. She didn't sound too pleased to hear from Aunt Anne. I wondered if she was still mad because Aunt Anne covered up for me about the dance.

"Yes, he is flying in a company plane and of course he will let you know," said Mother, getting more exasperated every second.

It made Dad mad to have Aunt Anne check up on what time he got home. She said she did it because families should be close to each other, but Dad said she worried about planes, especially unscheduled flights. Probably because of Grandfather. Once a thing like that happens to you, you never really lose the scar. Usually, soon after Dad got home, he would sigh and say, "Well, I guess I'd better punch Anne's Time Clock."

Mother spoke again after a long interval. "Anne, I wish you wouldn't work yourself into such a lather. You know that sort of thing is a lot of nonsense!" She sounded overemphatic.

I knew what Aunt Anne was talking about. She always swore she had this spooky sixth sense that made her "know" when something awful was going to happen. Like people dreaming about relatives dying and they die. Or wives calling their husbands and saying, "Don't get on that plane, it's going to crash!" And it crashes.

Mother was so matter-of-fact and sensible, I was surprised that she listened to it all the way through. I thought she'd say "Oh, *really*, Anne!" and hang up.

"I'm not *really* concerned," Mother was saying. Her voice was a little higher than it was when she started talking to Aunt Anne. "He's *not* very late. I didn't expect him before seven. I'm sure he'll walk in the door any minute."

Aunt Anne pulled out her whole bag of tricks. While she talked I watched Paul push his turtle around the tablecloth on a red stripe.

"It's too bad Hawaiian Eye doesn't have wheels," he murmured, intent, oblivious to everything around him.

It was seven forty-five. I found it impossible not to look at the clock when I was so hungry. *I* wouldn't be allowed to talk on the phone that long, I thought. Dad always said you never could tell who might be trying to reach us. I turned pleading eyes on Mother.

"— the minute he gets home!" she said, and slammed down the receiver.

"What a fuss-budget!" I said, eyeing the mashed potatoes.

I expected that Mother would answer "Mrs. Calamity Jane herself," or some such.

But, instead, she looked at me the way I'd been noticing all week, and when she spoke she sounded as though she was asking for serious advice from a grown-up friend.

"Anne thinks I ought to call the Providence office," she said. "What do you think?"

Her voice gave me goose pimples all over. I could hear that she was afraid something might have happened to Daddy's plane; and I realized that she hadn't sounded cross because dinner was late, she sounded that way because she was scared about Daddy; and, most of all, I suddenly understood that she must have worried herself sick a thousand times that I never knew. The way Paul didn't know that very minute.

She used to protect me, reassure me gently that everything was all right. This time she was asking for reassurance from me.

I felt dizzy and off balance. How could I know better than Aunt Anne? If Mother called the office at least she would talk to another adult; they would tell her what to think.

"I heard thunder a while ago," I said. "I think you'd better call."

"I hate to be the kind of wife that fusses over every little thing," said Mother. "I don't like to embarrass Daddy at the office."

"Listen to that wind," I said. The loose shutter banged and banged. I didn't see how Mother could act so calm. "Maybe something queer has happened," I said. "It's after eight o'clock."

Mother got out the phone book. She seemed shrunken and pitiful. I didn't like to look at her, so I stared at Paul.

"Our Daddy always gets home on Friday nights," Paul whispered to Hawaiian Eye. "Sometimes he gets home *this* way," he pushed the turtle between the salt and pepper, "— and sometimes he gets home *that* way" (around the milk pitcher) "— but he always gets home Friday nights. He tells Aunt Anne it's a matter of prin-ciple with him."

Mother was dialing. "I feel like such an old worry-wart!" she said, trying to smile at me. "But we'll both feel better when they tell us — Oh, yes. My husband, Mr. Frost, and your treasurer were scheduled to fly to New York this afternoon on your company plane. I'd like to inquire —"

"When he gets home —" Paul droned on, "— he picks me up and he says, 'Neither snow, nor sleet, nor gloom of night is ever going to stop your old Daddy-o from always getting home to you on —' "

"SHUT UP!" I shouted. I couldn't stand his gibbering.

Mother snapped her fingers for us to be quiet. I could hear a man's voice, but not his words.

Suddenly Mother gasped. The sound made an electric shock spread across my back. Even Paul looked up. Mother whispered, "Thank you," and leaned her head against the wall.

I snatched the phone from her and listened, but there was only the dial tone.

"What did he say?" I asked. "What's wrong?"

To look at her made me shiver. She was holding one hand flat across her stomach.

"Oh, dear," said Paul. "Are you going to —"

"It's all right, Paul," said Mother. She stood up straight and pulled down her sweater. "Now, children," she said, like a teacher, "Daddy's going to be a little late —" she took a deep breath, the way you do when you feel sick and need air, "— a little late for dinner. So I think it would be better if you ate."

"It's about time," said Paul, rudely.

Did Mother really think I could eat? My stomach felt swollen with empty misery, not hungry any more.

I would have given anything in the world to be like Paul — oblivious, protected — the way Mother used to let me be. But I couldn't be that way any more. During the last two miserable weeks I had learned that you have to be honest with yourself and face up to unpleasant facts squarely.

"I think I'll wait and eat with you and Daddy," I said, in a calm, even voice.

I could feel that Mother wanted to share her worry with me, as though I were a contemporary, the way she must have wanted to other times that I didn't understand.

"Why don't you tell me about the plane," I said. "Two heads are better than one."

"All right," said Mother. She put a plate of food in front of Paul. He started to shovel it in. "I talked to a salesman who was just leaving the office. He said that the company plane was scheduled to take off at three thirty and that Daddy and the treasurer got up and left a sales meeting at three o'clock to go to the airport." Her tone was assured and supersensible, even cheery.

That was what you did when something went wrong. You acted as though everything was fine and dandy. You helped each other best that way. "Mother," I said, "I'm absolutely certain —"

The telephone interrupted me.

"Oh, thank God!" said Mother. She put her palms flat against her cheeks. "I was so worried!"

"I'll get it!" said Paul, rising.

"No you won't!" I said, holding him down by the shoulders. "Let Mother talk to him." Relief flooded through me and loosened the knots in my stomach.

"Get off my back!" said Paul. "Mo-other!"

I held my hand over his mouth and looked at Mother.

But her eyes did not show relief. They were angry, scared, disappointed. "Oh, damn it, Anne!" she said. "I know he always calls when he's late. But this time he hasn't." She crashed the receiver onto the cradle.

"Oooom!" mumbled Paul, rolling furious eyes upward at me.

Mother sat down at the table and rested her head on her hands so that her fingertips stuck up through her brown hair. I remembered how Daddy always said that the top of her head and the top of mine were indistinguishable and distinguished. I tried not to think about Daddy.

Paul wrenched loose and drew in a deep breath so that I knew he was going to let out a screech. I couldn't let him.

"Paul," I wheedled, in my best baby-sitter voice. *"Let's* give Hawaiian Eye his dinner!"

He released the air slowly. "What'll we feed him?" he asked suspiciously.

I opened the refrigerator door and cut a sliver of raw meat. Paul snatched it. He put the turtle and the meat on Daddy's empty plate.

Daddy's plate must have reminded him. He looked at me with troubled brown eyes. "I should think Daddy would of been home by now," he said.

My breath caught and I glanced sideways at Mother. "He's going to be a little late," I told him gently. "Keep looking at Hawaiian Eye."

It was impossible not to remember how Grandfather had left Aunt Anne and little Daddy. I tried to keep out of my mind — Josie and little Paul.

Paul watched the turtle roll his yellow-rimmed eyes forward at the meat.

Mother hadn't moved. I took a bottle of cocktail sherry from the cabinet over the refrigerator and poured a juice glass full and set it down in front of her. I had trouble not looking at the clock. Mother sipped the sherry.

"Oooo —" Paul made a satisfied sound in his throat. He snatched the turtle up. There was nothing left on Daddy's plate except a spot of bright blood.

"I hope Daddy doesn't mind blood," said Paul. "What happened to Daddy's plane? Isn't he going to get home?"

"Don't you remember how Daddy always gets home?" I reminded him. "How neither snow, nor sleet, nor gloom of night —" It was too hard to say. "I hope Hawaiian Eye doesn't get heartburn," I said, shifting ground.

"How could he get hot-burn from cold food?" said Paul, scathingly. He shivered a little in his pajamas and rubbed his chest. "You know it's very sleety outside. Do you remember in March when the wings of the DC-7 iced up and —"

"Honey, Mother called the office," I said. "Remember? Everything is all right." I wondered if they phoned you when it wasn't, and how soon they phoned.

Paul started to speak again.

"You know what Hawaiian Eye would *really* enjoy now," I told him, "— is a nice big bath in the kitchen sink."

Paul groaned with pleasure. "Oh, Josie," he said. "You really have a passion for him, don't you?" He didn't wait for an answer.

I thanked heaven he was gone. I couldn't have stood another minute of it. I didn't like to think how many times Mother must have felt that way about me.

I stared at the spot on Daddy's plate. It was drying with a dark crust around the edges, like a scab. Black awfulness closed in on me.

Mother must have been watching my face.

"You know what I've been thinking," she said in a cheerful, chatty tone. "He might have decided to spend the night in Providence." She got up and looked around for a cigarette and lit one with a crisp snap of the match.

"I was thinking the same thing," I answered, brightly. "There are so many alternatives. Maybe the planes couldn't fly and he took a bus. Maybe he drove with someone."

But we both knew he would have called long ago.

There was no sound in the room except Paul running water in the sink, and even if I didn't want to I had to think about Daddy and the droll way he had of looking over the top of his pipe while he was lighting it. He almost had a dimple, but not quite.

Mother was thinking too, and her face didn't look good either. I saw her glance at the radio and I thought she was going to turn it on, but she didn't.

"I expect he's having a sandwich and a beer somewhere right now, while he's waiting for his turn at the phone," I said, in a brisk, brittle voice.

"That's right," said Mother, sociably. "When

everything's tied up by bad weather it can be terribly tiresome to get to a phone."

She pushed the sherry glass toward me. There was half an inch of amber liquid left in the bottom and I drank it. It burned all the way down, but it helped.

I turned the glass in my hand. It was not that Daddy was so exceptional or anything. He was really sort of ordinary. But I thought about the day I had the flu, when Daddy brought me some African violets. He said the sun on them would be like summer, and I would get well because summer was my best time.

"You know," said Mother, half rising, "we never checked to see if the phone was out of order. He could have been calling and calling —"

"Anne called," I said.

"Yes," she said. "That's right." She sat down.

"If there's one thing Hawaiian Eye is wild about," said Paul, "it's a really full bath in the —"

The phone rang.

"Round he goes," said Paul, splashing, "and down he dives —"

Mother and I looked at each other. The second ring stabbed the hush.

"I just know it's Aunt Anne again," I said. I prayed it wasn't . . . anything else. "Why don't you let me talk to her this time?"

Mother nodded and I picked up the receiver.

"Down he dives to the bottom —" said Paul, "— and up he comes —"

"Hello?" I said. My voice was a whisper.

"Kitten?" I heard. My eyes flooded.

"It's Daddy!" I said. I must have sounded like Easter morning.

Mother put her hands over her face.

"Where are you?" I asked.

"In town," he said. "At the station."

"He's h-here at the station," I said. I started to cry.

"Tut tut tut," he said. "Don't you know that neither snow, nor sleet, nor gloom of night can ever stop your old Daddy-o —"

"Owww!" I wailed, really letting go.

"I didn't mean to worry you," he said, concerned. "But I must say, I have a bone to pick with you and Peter."

"What b-bone?" I asked.

"When we got to the airport we decided it was insane to fly in this weather, especially in a company plane. So we just barely caught the New York train from Providence."

"He took the train," I told Mother, who was looking much better. I thought she might want the telephone, but she shook her head.

"— I had to change in New Haven to the seven forty-five local," Daddy was saying. "I dialed our number for fifteen whole minutes, from seven thirty to seven forty-five. If you and Peter —"

"Me and Peter!" I exclaimed. "It was your beloved sister Anne!"

Mother's face was a sight to see.

Daddy groaned. "I might have known," he said. "I called that number, too, and thought unprintable things about Priscilla."

"Is that Daddy?" asked Paul.

"Look," said Daddy. "I see a cab coming and I'm going to grab it."

"Can I talk to him?" asked Paul, leaving the sink.

"He hung up," I said.

"You did that on purpose!" said Paul, stamping his foot. "You're vile! You never let me talk to anyone!"

"You might have let him say 'hello,' " said Mother, noticing Paul for the first time in hours.

"But Daddy hung up," I argued. After all I'd done all evening to keep Paul quiet! "How was I supposed to —"

The sound of rushing, cascading water interrupted us.

"Paul!" I said. "The sink!"

Hawaiian Eye streamed over the side like a black barrel flowing over Niagara Falls. Paul shrieked and rolled his eyes upward until only the whites showed. "Stupid turtle!" I said. Paul shrieked louder.

"Really, children," said Mother, turning the water off and pulling the plug, "haven't I had enough this evening?"

Don't "children" me, I thought, helping her mop up.

"Oh, not again!" said Mother.

The phone was ringing.

"You *know* it's Aunt Anne this time," I said.

"I simply will not speak to her again," said Mother, flopping onto a kitchen chair, letting her arms hang down straight like a Raggedy Ann. "Give Paul a turn," she said wearily.

"You can answer it," she said to Paul.

"I can?" he said. He stopped yelling, but he couldn't help the sobbing hiccups. "Hello?" he said into the phone. "Aunt Anne? Oh, Aunt Anne, it's been the most terrible evening." He snuffled and examined his dripping turtle.

I heard Aunt Anne asking him hysterical questions.

"Mother!" I said, shocked. "Aunt Anne thinks . . . it sounds as if —"

"See we have this turtle," Paul was saying, "and his name is Hawaiian Eye because his eyeballs are so Hawaiian —"

"Tell Aunt Anne your father is on his way up from the station," said Mother, in an utterly-sick-of-Aunt-Anne tone of voice.

"Mother," I said, accusingly, "you should have called her the minute we heard from Daddy."

"I suppose so," said Mother. "But she gets me to the point where I'm beyond caring." She ran her finger along the red stripe on the tablecloth. "If she hadn't spent twenty minutes trying to work me into hysterics, tying up the phone while your father was calling . . . she wouldn't have had to worry either." Mother looked at me miserably. "You know this isn't the first time," she said.

"Hawaiian Eye hasn't met Daddy," Paul was saying.

I leaned over him so that I could talk into it without taking it away from him. "Aunt Anne?" I said. "Daddy is almost home. He took the train. I'm sure he'll call you after he's had something to eat."

I heard a broken "Thank you, child. I'm

sorry to be such a bother," as I straightened up again.

I could tell from Mother's expression that she wasn't too pleased with herself.

I thought, "suffering fools gladly" doesn't seem to be working too well.

"She can't help worrying about Daddy," I said. "You can't help loving someone, can you?" I noticed that I didn't feel numb any more. "You can't just turn it off at your convenience." When I heard myself say it I realized that this question had been in my mind every minute since the dance.

But Mother looked at me blankly; she wasn't up to an involved philosophical discussion.

We heard the scrapy-jingly sound of Daddy's key in the lock. In a minute he'd walk into the front hall, bringing the smell of outdoors and pipe smoke with him.

Mother disappeared, followed by Paul. Mother has the "loving someone" solved, I thought. Better than Aunt Anne.

Sometimes when you've been upset, you see things extra clearly: I knew that Daddy was unusually important to Aunt Anne, perhaps because Grandfather died while they were still young and Grammy was never too practical. Aunt Anne didn't have anyone to tell her how to keep Daddy from being quite so important. Even Uncle Jack couldn't keep Daddy (and Daddy's whole family) from being a little too important. She was always so terrified of suddenly losing him too.

But if you look at the person you love through worried eyes (or through romantic eyes) you get hurt. The answer, if you can learn young enough, is to look with your own clear everyday eyes. No fancy filters.

Aunt Anne was too old to learn that now. Dad should understand. Mother should make allowances.

He should call immediately so that she would feel she mattered and wasn't just a great big anxious nuisance.

"Daddy-o!" I shouted.

Daddy came in and kissed the top of my distinguished head. I pirouetted happily, so that my pleated skirt stood out like a dancer's.

I felt so good, that minute, that it had been almost worth feeling bad, and I knew for sure that the worst feeling was no feeling at all, to be numb the way I'd been since the dance.

"What's happened to Josie?" Dad asked Mother. "She's smiling! No! I do believe she's laughing!"

I started to giggle, then I remembered Aunt Anne.

"Daddy —" I said.

"Let's *eat!*" he said.

He *had* to call Aunt Anne. "Daddy," I said. "First you have to —"

"Second," he said. "First of anything I guess I'd better punch Anne's Time Clock." He still had on his soaking coat.

"Don't be too hard on Anne," said Mother, all happy smiles, all her warm self again. "You know how she is about you. I expect she's had a terrible evening."

I had the annoying feeling that all this had happened before to these three people. Over and over. And that they had always weathered it. In a way, they knew all along that everything would be all right. More than I did. Because it always had been.

"Of course you're not," I heard Daddy say. "You're no trouble at all."

The heck with their generation!

I resolved that the following Friday night I'd leave all the brouhaha for Paul to handle. His technique was actually more effective than mine. As for myself, I intended to get to the basketball game with Peter. Come hell or high water!

6

If We Could Each
Give in a Little

As the weather turned warmer and we could
be out of doors, I fell into the habit of doing
more and more with Peter. Not that we were
anything special to each other. Not going
steady. I had no illusions. (Once bitten, twice
shy.) But when Peter wasn't around I'd start
looking for him. I'd look up whenever anyone came into the room. Without him I felt flat.
No fizz. By Memorial Day we had reached the
point where we understood that we would
check all our plans with each other.

And a good thing too, because on the last
Saturday each May we have a gala event in
our town called Opening Day. The tennis
courts and the swimming pool open for the
season with matches, races, and, in the evening, a big barbecue. Everyone goes to the
barbecue and Mother's idea of a very good time
was to go as-a-family.

Eating with Paul in public was becoming
increasingly sickening to me, and I resolved

not to have it happen again. I was searching my mind for an acceptable excuse, when it occurred to me to check with Peter.

"But that's the day of the dog show," said Peter, surprised that I even asked. "You'll be going up to Greenwich with me that day."

I remembered Peter telling me, several weeks earlier, that he had entered his dog, Spike, in the obedience trials. He had been training Spike all winter and had already shown him twice. If Spike won enough points in the Greenwich show, he would receive his certificate. Peter was sure Spike would qualify and he was terribly excited.

How could I possibly say no? Even Mother grudgingly saw it my way.

The morning of the show I was ready long before eight o'clock. (Greenwich was a forty-minute drive.) It was early; I thought I'd be safely gone before anyone got up. But it was not too early for Mother.

She padded after me in her slippers and robe, offering me orange juice and repeating like a broken record, "Josie, I do think it would be appropriate if we could turn up at the Opening Day barbecue as-a-family."

Theme with variations.

She didn't realize that the secret of her lack of success lay in those unattractive little words, as-a-you-know-what.

"We *may* get back from the dog show in time," I said, "and then again we may *not*."

I was in sole possession of the information that the dog show was over at five o'clock. (Peter had showed me the program inside his Virgil in Latin class one morning.) Plenty of time to get back for the barbecue, which started at six. Or, preferably, little enough time so that I could dawdle around on the way home from Peter's and arrive a tidy few minutes after Mother and Dad and Paul had left for the barbecue.

"I don't see why you can't be more definite," Mother said.

She was grouchy because she doesn't like to swim or play tennis the way Daddy does and so she wasn't going to have any fun all day and she saw the big social event of the evening fast slipping through her fingers.

Seeing Mother upset by Aunt Anne and by Daddy's late plane had made me want to be nicer to her. For the first time I really understood that Mother was a human being with problems and unhappinesses of her own, not just a person who was always right.

She had gotten up early to see me off, to be sure that I had a proper breakfast. There was a dark stain on her robe where she had spilled something and she had slept on her hair wrong so that it stuck out and she hadn't had time to put on any lipstick.

I wished that she was going to have a nicer day. I couldn't see that it was my responsibility, but, for the first time that I could remember, it touched me. It was on the tip of my tongue to suggest that she call a friend and drive up to Greenwich.

"What a shame Paul can't see the dog show, too," she said. "He'd love —"

Oh, no! I thought. Thank heavens I didn't suggest anything.

"There they are!" I said. Just in time!

I got into the car happy, but it didn't last. As I live and breathe, Peter and his father were having it out about the selfsame Opening Day. Dr. Stern, it seemed, considered himself a star tennis player and he couldn't stand to miss seeing a minute of it and the first tennis match started at eleven o'clock. They hardly stopped squabbling long enough to say good morning to me.

Peter's tune was, "How'd I know the dog show was going to be the same day as the (pause) Opening Day?" (I could hear him leave out some unspeakable word in the pause.)

And Dr. Stern snapped back with, "I said I'd take you, and I'm taking you, but don't expect me to be pleasant about it."

Wow! It sounded like home.

I could see the whole day was going to be a total loss.

One thing for sure, no one was embarrassed but me. I squirmed down small between them. It was so much like me and Mother that I didn't know whether to laugh or cry.

Peter's dog, a pint-size Lassie, ended up in my lap by default. Spike was a Shetland sheepdog, blackish brown, with a stiff white ruff, a white stripe on his nose, and a white tip to his foxy tail. I stroked him and talked to him and pretended not to hear the bickering.

The ruckus between Peter and his father came to a head around eight forty-five when we began to see signs saying DOG SHOW TODAY. The sight of the signs made Dr. Stern boil up all over again.

The show was on a big estate. Far off, across a flower-dotted meadow beside a red barn, we saw lots of activity: a hamburger stand and booths with doggie things for sale. We turned onto a dirt road and stopped behind a line of cars, bumper to bumper, for at least a quarter of a mile. Way ahead in the parking lot, row on row of cars reflected spots and flashes of sunshine.

Dr. Stern blew his top. "We'll park in the meadow," he announced. "We'll never get out of that mess."

"By five o'clock —" Peter began.

"Five o'clock, ha!" said Dr. Stern. "All I agreed was that you show your dog."

Peter sucked in his breath. "That's not fair," he said. "I wanted to watch the exhibition trials at one thirty."

"Your class starts at nine thirty. After that, home!"

"The Best of Breed isn't until four."

"You get to show your dog in the morning, I get to watch the tennis in the afternoon. Fair?"

"But Jo wanted to see the afternoon part." His voice was shaky. "That's when they show the Shelties. Jo —" he appealed.

"I'll do whatever is convenient," I said. Not that I'd changed my mind about the barbecue, but I was beginning to think that I didn't have the intestinal fortitude to listen to an All Day Hassle. (Come to think of it, that's one of Dad's pet phrases.)

"See?" said Dr. Stern.

I felt like a traitor.

Peter's back stiffened. I could feel that he was seething inside. He almost couldn't sit another minute.

How come we all feel we've lost, I wondered, when nobody won.

Dr. Stern was turning onto some tire tracks in the meadow. If I'd been with my family I'd have started humming the Chopin Funeral March. Sometimes that sort of thing breaks it up. But I wasn't too sure of Dr. Stern.

We heard the yipping and yelping of dogs already at the show and Spike pricked up his ears. As soon as Dr. Stern found a good place to park, before he even turned off the motor, Peter flung open the door. He was so mad he couldn't wait for anything, just started running blindly across the field. His long legs covered ground fast and Spike streaked alongside him, a brown and white blur. I thought how Spike would look herding sheep, dashing this way and that — suddenly I saw Peter go down.

Dr. Stern and I started to run, but Peter was up before we got to him. He lifted one foot, which seemed to be all mixed up with a piece of board, and looked over his shoulder (to see if his father had noticed, I thought). He pulled the board free of his foot. By the time we reached him he was walking along, gingerly, to show nothing was wrong.

"Just tripped over a board," he grumbled. "Let's not make a federal case —"

Dr. Stern picked up the board. A great rusty nail stuck through it.

"This go into your foot?" he asked.

"Not really," said Peter.

"Well, either it did or it didn't," said Dr. Stern. "Take off your shoe." He made Peter sit. "If you'd wear proper shoes —" he scolded, "— instead of these silly sneakers —" (just like Mother) "— this sort of thing wouldn't happen."

But I saw that he was gentle and I heard that he was upset and concerned about Peter. Probably he was thinking it was partly his fault. Which it was.

I felt definitely . . . extra. So I went after Spike. He was running round and round in zany, crazy-dog circles, getting burrs in his coat that Peter had slaved over, combing, brushing, and combing again.

I called him, but he wouldn't come. It was the thing he did worst. Finally I was able to grab the end of the leash. If he hadn't had his leash on I never would have caught him.

I tried to pick the burrs and twigs out of his ruff. He didn't exactly enjoy it, so I was glad when I saw Peter and his father standing up.

"I'll go right after the show," Peter argued loudly.

"We can't fool around with the possibility of tetanus, son," said Dr. Stern. "And there may be something in your foot. If we wait until it starts swelling we'll be in trouble." He was trying hard to be nice.

"You're glad!" said Peter. His voice cracked. "You want me to miss the show. So you can get back in time for the stupid Opening Day tennis!"

"You know that isn't so," said Dr. Stern, quietly, without any yelling. "I'm sorry, son, but as a physician I have to insist on taking you back to the office to get that fixed up." He put his hand on Peter's shoulder.

"Let go of me!" shouted Peter. "I'm not going anywhere!" He sat down on the grass again. I could see that he was planning to die of tetanus right there in the field before he'd go with his father.

His long legs with his knees sticking up reminded me of a grasshopper.

I never saw a boy cry, but I knew that Peter was going to.

I knew so well how Peter felt (from battles with Mother) that I almost had to sit down too. But, for once, I was enough outside of it to see that if they'd work together on solving the problem instead of separately on each winning his own side of the fight, they might get somewhere.

Peter sat and Dr. Stern stood.

If they could each give in a little —

"You're both being silly!" I said, a little too loud. My voice squeaked because I was scared of Dr. Stern. "Get up, Peter!" I said. "You're wasting time."

They stared at me, as surprised as if Spike had spoken.

"Why do you have to go all the way home?" I asked. "Why don't you go in to Greenwich? Why can't you get the shot there?"

"We *could* do that," said Dr. Stern, slowly. "I'd be willing to go to the hospital emergency room."

Peter didn't budge. His hands, with their long fingers, dangled between his knees. "We'd miss our turn," he said dully.

"You're being stupid and stubborn," I said. "I'll stand in line with Spike. Leave me here."

"Fine!" said Peter, jumping up. "Ouch!" he added.

"Oh, I don't know at all," said Dr. Stern. He had no daughters and I could see he was way beyond his depth.

"I stay at dog shows by myself all the time," I said brightly.

"What could happen to her?" asked Peter. "If you *have* to show him, Jo, on the recall —"

"Hurry!" I said. "You'll be back. I'll get on the end of the line."

I watched them go.

What I didn't know was that the judge arranges the order of the show. He had Spike listed fourth in a class of thirty dogs. He was nice, but he said that he wasn't allowed to change it.

There was nothing to do but stand there, fourth in line for Obedience Trials: Novice Class A. Me, Josie, who never went to a dog show or even had a dog in my whole life. I took a deep breath of the flower-fragrant air, but it didn't help any. So I crossed my fingers and chanted to myself over and over, like a charm, "Please, Peter, come back in time. I need you."

Every so often I went up on tiptoe to see if I could catch sight of the car with Peter and his father. I imagined they weren't having too joyous a time of it, considering how it had been on the drive over.

One good thing, I had gotten to know Spike pretty well in the car. I looked down at him. He was pulling on the leash because the Obedience Trial line had moved up. The first dog, a black dachshund, trotted into the ring. Novice Class A had begun.

I shivered.

The ring, circled with posts and white ropes, measured about twice the size of our living room. People gathered around to watch. The judge and two helpers stood on the fresh-cut grass, holding clipboards with white papers that curled backward in the breeze.

I remembered how Peter had told me to watch the other dogs carefully.

An elderly man was showing the dachshund. How the little dog loved him! He never took his eyes off the man's face. He walked close at the man's left heel, on a loose leash. When the judge told the man to run, the dog ran; when the man stood still, the dog sat by his side, without the man saying a word, or pulling on the leash. I could have hugged the little dog for doing it so well.

In the novice class you do everything on the leash except one thing — the recall. Peter worried about the way Spike did the recall. He had talked about it in the car on the way over, whenever there was a temporary truce.

"Isn't that Peter Stern's dog?" asked a voice near my ear.

"Oh!" I said. "Yes. This is Peter's dog."

A lady about Mother's age stood beside me, wearing slacks and a tailored shirt. Her brownish-gray hair coiled into a braided bun.

"Peter and I go to the same dog-training class," she said pleasantly.

I knew how Peter looked forward to going every Tuesday evening.

"We are both hoping to win enough points in this show to qualify for our certificates. Then we graduate to the Wednesday class."

She didn't say, "What are you doing with Peter's dog? How come he isn't here?" or anything nosy like that. So I told her everything that had happened.

"Gracious!" she said. "Peter has worked so hard. I suppose you have been training Spike too?"

"I don't even know how to unhook the leash," I said, trying to sound flip and off-hand because I was getting closer to tears every minute that Peter didn't come.

The line moved up one and a German shepherd paced into the ring.

"Oh, dear," she said. "Well, let's show you a few things."

She did.

"It's not enough," she said, handing me back Spike's leash. "But it's better than nothing." We got into line again.

"You did everything but the recall," I said.

"That's done . . . off the leash," she said. She frowned vaguely. "Maybe Peter will get back."

In the ring the judge examined the German shepherd.

"Almost my turn," she said. Her dog was a honey-colored girl cocker whom Spike knew and liked. Their tails were wagging up a storm.

"I'll probably see you around this afternoon," said the lady, smoothing out the cocker's silky ears with her pocket comb. Spike wasn't helping much.

"We have to go after this class," I said. "Dr. Stern has to . . . get back."

"Goodness! You'll miss the best part!" she said, standing up. "You shouldn't go home so early."

I was beginning to think that home was a place I never should have left. Barbecue or no barbecue.

"Well —" she said, "good luck. I'm on now." She walked the cocker into the ring.

"Ready?" asked the judge.

She nodded.

I should have said good luck to her. She was so kind. But all I could think was, I'm next after her.

With no one to talk to I felt cold and shaky again. The crowds were bigger every minute and the people were quiet and serious about the dogs. A few had noticed that I was next. They looked at their programs and then at Spike.

The only real hope was that Peter might come back and that hope was rapidly vanishing.

I knew I should keep watching the ring, but I was all the time looking for the car instead. I never dreamed it would take so long.

I saw that the lady in slacks was doing the recall, the last exercise for each dog. She made the cocker sit at one end of the ring. Then she used the hand signal meaning "stay": palm flat, in front of the dog's nose.

(Peter said that Spike did it this far properly.)

She unsnapped the leash from the cocker's collar and walked way to the other end of the

112

ring and turned around facing the dog, who was supposed to sit there for one whole minute.

(Spike even did this part right.)

When the judge nodded, she called her dog. The cocker ran to her and sat down in front of her. "Exercise finished," said the judge. Only then did the cocker jump up to be praised. Everybody clapped.

(As I understood it Spike *ran* all right, but he didn't necessarily run to Peter. Without the leash to restrain him, he took off in any direction that looked attractive.)

I imagined Spike tearing around the ring in front of all those serious people . . . me chasing him . . . dashing out of the exit . . . dodging through the crowds —

To hide my face I bent over Spike with my pocket comb. At least Peter could be proud of the way Spike looked.

"Number four, Shetland sheepdog. 'Spike.' Owner: Mr. Peter Stern," the judge announced over his megaphone.

I took one last desperate look around for Peter.

"Don't you worry," said the cocker lady, coming out of the ring. She must have understood from my face what I was thinking. "I'll block the exit at the end," she said. "In case he . . . gets loose."

"Please, Spike," I whispered. "Do it right for me —"

Spike was watching me with alert brown eyes, tail wagging. Peter had told me he loved to be shown.

The lady gave me a nudge.

I was numb as I walked into the ring. I didn't know what made my legs go.

The crowd hushed.

"Are you ready?" asked the judge.

I nodded, as I had seen the others do.

"For-ward!" he said.

"Spike! Hee-eel!" I commanded.

I walked around the ring. Spike paced at my left heel.

I was past caring what happened. I said to myself, "In fifteen minutes this will be over." At the rope faces were flesh-colored blurs; clothing, flashes of color.

"Slow!" said the judge.

I walked very slowly. Spike slowed right down with me. He watched my face every second.

"Fast!"

I ran.

Spike ran too. By my left heel, as he should.

"Halt!"

I stood still. I hardly dared look.

Spike was sitting. Almost touching my left leg. Still watching me. He was perfect.

"Figure of eight!" said the judge.

Two stewards came into the ring and stood six feet apart with their arms folded. Spike and I looped between them briskly and correctly.

"Exercise finished!" said the judge.

A storm of clapping burst from the crowd.

I fell to my knees and gathered Spike into my lap. "Good fel-low," I crooned, rocking him back and forth, over and over.

"Stand for examination!" said the judge. He was smiling.

Spike stood proud in his white ruff, hand-some the way Peter had bathed and brushed him. People in the crowd whispered and pointed. How they loved him! How I wished Peter could see him!

"The recall!" said the judge.

My heart hammered. I wanted to say, "He's been so good. We've tried so hard. Can't you judge what he's done? Couldn't you wait for Peter?"

But I led Spike to the end of the ring. The cocker lady blocked the exit.

"Sit!" I said to Spike.

He sat.

"Stay!" I gave the hand signal, palm flat against his moist, black, inquisitive nose. My fingers fumbled and trembled with unsnap-ping the hook on the leash from the loop on Spike's collar.

I walked to the other end of the ring, star-ing down at the bumpy turf, and turned facing Spike, holding the leash in both hands as I had seen other handlers do.

No one said a word. Even the dogs beside the ring didn't seem to be barking.

My back was against the ropes.

Spike was still sitting at the other end of the ring. His ears drooped as though he had been punished. I remembered Peter saying that Spike always had hurtsy feelings when he was told to "stay."

I thought the judge would never tell me to call him in.

Suddenly Spike's ears shot up. He started to break from the sit. I wondered what he had seen behind me, but didn't dare turn my head.

An interesting girl dog? He sat back properly.

"Do the recall!" said the judge.

"Spike! Co-ome!" I commanded.

Spike streaked across the ring, brown and white silky hair low to the ground. He came barrelling in, arrow-straight, toward me. I thought he wasn't even going to stop, but he skidded to a rakish, quivering "sit" in front of me, shaking violently with excitement.

"Exercise finished!" said the judge.

"GRAB HIM!" said a voice behind me. It was Peter.

I barely caught the tip of Spike's tail as he tried to take off. The crowd, in an uproar of clapping, started to laugh. But friendly.

"Good old Jo," said Peter, pounding me on the back.

"Oh, Peter," I said, handing him the squirming Sheltie, "you should have seen —"

"We *did* see," said Peter. "You walked right by me."

I remembered the blur of faces.

"Spike didn't see me until the recall," said Peter. "I purposely stayed out of sight. Then I was afraid he might bolt —"

I remembered Spike's ears going up.

"— so I stood right behind you. In case you needed help catching him."

"Spike!" I said. "You didn't come because you liked me. You thought you could get through to Peter. I'm offended."

But I wasn't.

"Good girl!" said Peter's father, squeezing through the crowd. He put an arm about each of us. He and Peter seemed to have made up.

"I wish I could figure some way for you kids to stay."

"That's all right, Dad," said Peter. "Spike has earned his certificate."

"I might have another idea," I said.

"Not another!" said Dr. Stern, in mock awe.

But I was beginning to see how we could all win and nobody lose. Even Mother (if she'd cooperate).

"My mother would like me to . . . be at the barbecue this evening," I said to Peter.

He got the message that he was supposed to invite me and he sort of bumped into me sideways so that I understood that we would be going together.

In a way it was as-a-family and in a way it wasn't. I would go, but I wouldn't sit with Paul. It depended on how you looked at it, but I figured maybe Mother would trade barbecue attendance for transportation.

"Dr. Stern," I said. "Why don't I see if Mother could drive up to get us at five o'clock?"

"Fine!" said Dr. Stern, beaming at me. He showed me a phone. "I'll save a big table," he said, inspired. "We can all sit together."

Peter made a face as though he was going to throw up.

I felt the way he looked, but I dialed and (think of the devil) it was Paul who answered the phone.

"Is Mother in a good mood?" I asked.

"Foul," said Paul. "She just talked to Aunt Anne."

There was a scuffle over the phone.

"Hello?" said Mother. "Josie?"

"Mother," I said. "If I scratch your back will you scratch mine?"

"Whaaaaat?" said Mother.

"Mother, Peter and I would very much like to come to the barbecue tonight and the Sterns would like to sit with us too," I said, as though I were accepting a formal invitation.

"Oh!" said Mother. "How *nice*. I think Dr. Stern is *so* attractive —"

"Mother, please!" I said. I covered the earpiece with my hand until I thought she had finished burbling about Dr. Stern.

"One other little thing, Mother," I said. "Could you come up and get us?"

There was a silence. Peter was watching me with anxious eyes through the glass front of the booth. He was still holding Spike.

"Come now?" asked Mother.

"At five o'clock," I said. "See, Dr. Stern —"

"It's a wonderful idea!" said Mother. "We're not doing a thing. We'll be right up."

"We?" I asked. But I didn't really have to.

"Paul will love the dogs," said Mother.

"Ohhhh," I answered.

"Maybe Dr. Stern could reserve a table," she continued happily.

"He will," I said.

"We'll be needing ten places," said Mother. "Anne and Jack and Priscilla are joining us. Anne called to say that Henry won't be with them this weekend after all, so she's not going to spend the money on going in to New York. I hope it won't be too much family for the Sterns."

Not for the Sterns, I thought.

"Josie?" she said. "Are you there? Is everything all right?"

I remembered how woebegone she had looked in her robe and slippers because everyone was going to have a wonderful spring Saturday but her.

"Everything's fine, Mother," I said. "Hurry along up. You'll love it. And . . . so will Paul."

I hung up and turned to Peter's father. "You can go home," I said. "Go *fast*."

"Josie says I can go home now," said Dr. Stern, solemnly, to Peter.

I blushed. "I mean . . . you can get home by the time the tennis starts."

"I understand completely," said Dr. Stern. "I'll go home and watch the tennis and save a table for the Frosts and the Sterns —"

"— and also my Aunt Anne and my Uncle Jack and my cousin Priscilla, if you don't mind too much," I said, blushing furiously again.

Peter started to laugh.

"Don't pay any attention to him. He has no manners," said Dr. Stern, soothing me. "It will be our pleasure to dine with your aunt and uncle." He gave Peter a dirty look. "And your mother will come for you at five?"

"She's coming right now," I said. It was my turn to look meaningfully at Peter. "With *Paul*."

Peter stopped laughing abruptly.

"I apologize for my son," said Dr. Stern, slipping Peter something from his pocket.

Peter gave a hop of pleasure on his good foot. "Thanks, Dad," he said. "Hope you win your match, too," he called, almost shyly, after his father.

The noon sun shone yellow above the meadow and barn. Spike pranced between us on dainty white feet. My day was beginning to fizz.

"Let's watch them judge the collies," said Peter. He snapped a daisy from its stem and handed it to me.

"Let's get a hamburger on the way," I said, fastening the flower into my hair with my barrette.

"Let's buy Spike —" he looked at the bill his father had given him and his eyes got bigger "— a silver collar!"

"With rubies!"

"Emeralds!" He took my hand.

"Sapphires!" Spike and I ran beside him as he hobbled happily across the spring-soft grass.

It was the best day I ever had with Peter.

7

Going to Almost Everything Together

Going places (with Peter to take me) was much more fun than staying home with my family. For the first time in my life I was getting around. It was fun. I became quite the butterfly.

But I knew that sooner or later some of my new activities were bound to make my parents nervous. Sure enough, by the middle of June the atmosphere had become too tense to tolerate and one Friday evening we had the inevitable blowup.

I was late to dinner and I slid into my chair so fast that it tipped. I had been singing up a happy storm in the shower and it was hard to simmer down.

Dad started to work up a humorous-sarcastic bit about "Aren't we coming in a little hot? Let's not have any more crash landings —"

There were times when I honestly felt I could do without my parents. I cut him off. "T.G.I.F.!" I announced.

"What?" said Mother.

"Thank God it's Friday!"

"Jo-sie," Mother warned.

"Peter says it all the time," I said.

There followed the icy silence that had accompanied every mention of Peter's name all spring. It made me feel bad, but I refused to show it. I tried to get around it by acting flippant.

"I'm going over after dinner to listen to Peter's ham radio," I stated.

Everyone drew in a deep breath. Including me. I felt sorry Paul wasn't home. He made a good buffer.

"I have no homework," I said defensively, "and it's the next to last week of school."

Mother and Dad looked at each other to see who was going to take the opener. Dad was chicken.

"Josie," said Mother, staring with great interest at the tines of her fork. "I thought you understood that we feel you are spending too much time with Peter."

I pushed my lower lip forward. This habit was replacing my rude stare. It was more subtle. Parents had to be pretty mad at a kid before they'd fuss about moving a lower lip a quarter of an inch. But I'd noticed that it got the message across.

"It's not that we don't *like* Peter," said Dad quickly.

"Not at *all*," said Mother.

"Pretty soon we'll be going to the shore anyway," I said. "Then I won't be seeing him at all."

"Your father and I think we should come to some agreement about this before we go," said Mother. "And not have it hanging fire all summer. Then you'll be over it —"

"Over *what?*" I asked. "You used to fuss because I never went out, and now you fuss because I do go out." I made a face to indicate that parents were hopeless cases and I tried to eat fast so that I could get out quickly.

"It's too much with one boy," said Mother. "Last winter you went to all the basketball games with him."

"He takes you to the movies," said Dad.

"He calls every evening."

"You sit in the basement with him for three hours every Friday night."

"No fair two against one!" I said, holding up my hands in mock defense, trying for a laugh.

I didn't get one.

"You go to all the parties and dances together," said Mother.

"His dog knows you," said Dad.

"He has your picture."

"Who?" I asked. "His dog?"

I remembered how I had my picture taken for Peter because I thought Henry might ask for one. But Mother didn't know that. She thought it was for Peter.

"The barbecue last month —"

"The dog show —"

"The splash party —"

"It's Friday nights in the basement that I really mind," said Dad to Mother. "Down there in that Black Hole of Calcutta —"

"Oh, no," said Mother. "I don't mind the basement. I mind her always being seen with Peter. No one else will ask her —"

"Where they're seen doesn't bother me," said Dad. "It's where they're not seen —"

Usually Dad is sweet and permissive. I can twist him around my little finger. But the subject of Peter brought out the tiger in him. While they argued I finished my stew.

I'd been going to Peter's Friday evenings since April, about two months. As soon as the basketball games ended he had time to practice up and get his ham license. He had set up his radio equipment in a corner of the basement and worked on it every spare minute, but of course he hadn't been allowed to go on the air until he passed the FCC radio amateurs tests. I always seemed to get involved with boys who were interested in math and physics and engineering.

In front of the transmitter and receiver there was an old piano bench. We sat there together. He received and sent messages and I wrote in the logbook. My handwriting was much nicer than Peter's and my part of the book looked beautiful, though Peter kept trying to impress me that accuracy was more important. It was thrilling to hear the other hams, sometimes from hundreds of miles away when it was a good night, and I didn't always get the exact information. Still, I was a real help. Often it needed two people.

The previous Friday Peter had spent the

whole evening on the roof adjusting the antenna. (That was hardly seeing too much of Peter, was it?) I stayed in the basement taking readings on the receiver. Peter said lots of ways it would have been better if I had been on the roof and he —

"— bad for her school work," Dad was saying.

"It can be upsetting when these . . . um . . . attachments are broken off," said Mother. "When they're over —"

"What's to be over?" I said, reaching for the salad. "Nothing's begun." I knew my smart-alecky attitude was irritating them, but it was the only way I could hold them off.

"It's not the end I mind," said Dad. "It's while it's going on."

"Nothing's going on," I said.

"It's not while it's going on I mind," said Mother. "It's the end."

Really folks, I thought. Get together. Make sense. For years the whooping and the keening had been about how I never went anywhere. Now that I was getting around, why did they knock it? I could count on Peter for everything. He took me everywhere. It was much simpler than worrying about a whole bunch of different boys.

"I guess I'm monogamous," I announced, expecting a laugh.

The old funny bones were tough to tickle. Neither one of them cracked a smile; instead — raised eyebrows.

"One tends to become more and more . . . involved," said Dad. He looked embarrassed. "Things tend to get . . . uh . . . out of hand."

"The trouble with going steady —" said Mother slowly.

"GOING STEADY!" I said. "Who said anything about GOING STEADY?" I dropped my spoon with a clatter. "You're crazy!"

So that was what they thought.

"You and Peter obviously have some sort of a . . . an understanding," said Mother. "It doesn't matter what you call it."

"It does *too*. We do *not*," I insisted.

"Clearly you do," said Mother.

"He calls me *up*. We *go* places. That's *all*," I continued desperately.

For once in my life I was telling the truth.

I remembered the horrible miserable things that Mother had said about Priscilla when she was going steady. Things that were none of Mother's business, things that had nothing to do with Peter and me. I knew that she was going to say them all over again, and she did.

"Please, Mother," I said, with one last attempt at humor. "Not while I'm eating."

It didn't even slow her down. To Mother, going steady is just one step from the altar. Or worse. She was objectionably graphic and explicit. Gruesomely physical. I didn't know which way to look. I never even thought of things like that about Peter.

Dad too. "No daughter of mine —" he kept saying. "I'll lock her up first." He talked about — oh, dear —

I felt my face getting red; I was prickly hot with shame I didn't deserve.

Nobody said anything; they sat and watched me.

"We weren't born yesterday," said Mother, after what seemed like forever.

She said it nicely and sympathetically, but I knew that both of them, because they had seen me blush, were sure they had hit the nail on the head.

It wasn't true. It was intolerable not to be believed. But I knew that I could protest a thousand years and they would smile knowingly on. I couldn't stand their faces.

I couldn't eat any more. I kept my hands under the table because they were shaking.

"I told Peter I was coming," I said, with as much composure as I could manage. "So if you'll excuse me, I believe I'll be getting along." I tossed my head.

They exchanged another glance.

"Well — forewarned is forearmed," said Mother.

"Ten thirty sharp," said Dad. "And don't forget what we talked about."

It wasn't the sort of thing you forgot in a hurry, I thought, as I walked down the hill from our house.

I didn't know exactly where I was going, but I didn't see how I could go to Peter's. I imagined Peter in his school shirt with the sleeves rolled up and his chino pants and big scuffed loafers. He was like a brother or a cousin to me.

With my very parents thinking such fantastic things about us, how could I look at him the same way? How could I go places with him? Did other people think those things about us? Most of all, what did Peter think? My face got red again.

I hated even the words "going steady" and no one was ever going to say them about me. It made me think of seniors at school in their dreary parked cars, not me and Peter eating hamburgers in the sunshine at the dog show.

"We're only fifteen years old," I said out loud. "I'd even be embarrassed to talk to Peter about someone *else* in our class going steady, let alone us. That's how involved we are, Dad."

I was passing a vacant house, so I walked up the short path from the street and sat on the front steps. In between my parents and Peter, I thought, not belonging either place, belonging in a place like this, alone and empty.

"What do they expect?" I argued with myself. "Should I go back to reading and daydreaming behind a shut bedroom door, like a twelve-year-old? Even put my thumb in my mouth and carry a blanket? Would you like that better, Mother?"

The evening was warm and sweet-smelling, but I hated it.

When we went to basketball games, Peter left me sitting with the girls and he went out to help in the locker room, if he wasn't playing. How scandalous!

Beside the steps a daisy grew tall and straight out of the unmown grass.

At the Spring Get-Together, when I made such a fool of myself over Henry, Peter picked up the pieces of my pride by dancing every dance with me all evening. "Isn't that terrible, Mother?" I said. "We were seen dancing together."

I fingered the perfect flower.

We went to a horrid movie, once, that embarrassed both of us. Part way through Peter said, "This is a grubby movie, Jo. Let's go get something to eat."

"Is that the kind of boy 'no daughter of mine' should go to the movies with, Dad?"

I had never thought before about much of any difference between going somewhere with Peter and going somewhere with one of the girls I knew. Thanks a lot, parents.

I jerked the flower head off its stem and tore the white petals and crushed the yellow center and scattered the broken pieces all over the steps.

"Dear Mother," I said, "and dear, dear Father. Look at the mess you've made."

With my chin in my hands I sat and looked at the mess.

"I refuse to go home," I said to myself after a while. "I refuse to give them the satisfaction.

"And I can't wander around the streets all night tearing up flowers like some kind of a nut.

"If I don't show up at Peter's he'll phone. He'll ask where I am and Dad will beat the bass drums and call out the vice squad. I'm not even free *not* to go."

I stood up and started back along the walk.

I had to go to Peter's because I had to tell him: "Guess what, Peter. I've got news. No

more movies . . . no more parties . . . no
more barbecues . . . no more ham radio . . .
and — get your dog away from me, Peter. My
father says I'm not allowed to know a dog that
well."

Peter's mother opened the door. She didn't
say much to me. "Josie's here," she called to
Peter.

"Tell 'er to c'mon down," I heard Peter say.

"Your father and I think it would be nice
if you came *up* for a change," she called to
him. "Remember?"

Peter's dog jumped up on me. Peter's
mother was watching. "Get off, Spike," I
said, pushing him away.

"Down here," called Peter, crossly.

I slipped past her into the basement and
Spike followed me down the stairs. His toe-
nails clicked on every step.

Peter was sitting in the middle of the piano
bench. A single light bulb dangled over his
head. When he heard me he moved over to
one side of the bench without turning his head.
He was busy tuning up the transmitter. The
filaments of the vacuum tubes glowed yellow
in the dark basement as they warmed. His
logbooks and a sharp pencil were set out,
ready for me to take down messages.

I remained standing behind him. I didn't
know how to begin.

"Let's get going," he said, looking back at
me. He seemed cross, but I didn't think it was
my fault. "You start out with the headphones,"
he said, holding them up.

I backed away from him.

"I'll let you use the mike later," he said. "When everything's tuned right."

"I'd rather sit here," I said, moving some wires aside on the tool table behind him. "You . . . go ahead."

He shrugged and went on fiddling, not looking at me, but talking.

"I wish you'd stick around this summer," he said, changing the subject suddenly. "We only have a couple more weeks before you go to Maine."

He looked so solid and everyday in his sweatshirt and levis and loafers, it made me feel weepy.

"Couldn't you stay here with your father for part of the time?" he asked. "You could do some baby sitting or something. Tell 'em you need the money."

I'd never give up a minute of my time at the shore for anyone. I could hardly wait to get there. Problems with parents, Peter, everybody would vanish with the first scent of sun-warmed wood and privet and salt air off the bay.

I was already living the glorious moment when we would throw open the front door and I would run to open the windows and shake the mothballs from the blankets and scatter my summer books all over the living room and take my sailing jacket down from its hook behind the kitchen door —

"Isn't there any way I can see you before September?" asked Peter.

He was hinting to be invited up. But, I thought, I wouldn't want to share the shore, not with Peter. I had never even shown my white stone to Peter. He wouldn't have known what it was all about. Some people didn't and some people did.

In any case I could hardly imagine Mother and Dad inviting him. Peter at the shore would be all they needed.

"I'll write," I said.

"It'll be a long summer," he answered. "Will you write every day?"

"I'll write whenever . . . I can," I said. I wondered if they would try to read our letters. My voice was trembling.

"What'sa matter, Jo?" he asked. He laid the microphone down on its side and spun around on the bench.

"Nothing."

"Something, I think," he said. "Come. Sit here."

I shook my head. This was the time to say the things I had planned about not coming any more, but I couldn't get started.

"Cheer up!" he said. "T.G.I.F.!" He looked around his little corner. "See. I'll make you a bracelet while the transmitter warms up."

Among the dark snarl of tools and grimy radio parts on the table were three reels of wire with bright-colored insulation.

"What's your favorite color?" he asked.

"Yellow." I smiled, because it was silly and childish to make a yellow bracelet.

"That's better," he said. He cut a yard length of yellow-covered wire. Spaghetti, the hams call it — a funny name, but perfect when you see a lot of it scrambled up together.

"Tomorrow we'll go to the pool in the morning," he said. "OK?" He stripped the insulation off a section of wire with his pocketknife. "And then we can have a hamburger. OK? And then I'll pick you up at your house around eight for the Senior High Concert. Smile!"

I tried hard. He was so nice.

He talked along about who we were going to try to contact during the evening and while he talked his long fingers worked the stiff wire in and out as he braided the three-strand yellow Turk's Head. It was gay and pretty and as I watched his familiar brown hands pulling the wire up and through, I began to relax and be more like my usual self. Hearing him talk on, even the boring parts, like the best voltage to use, made me feel safe and ordinary again. I slid down from the table and looked at the dials on the transmitter to see if they were steady and fiddled with the button on the mike.

"Here," said Peter. He was holding out the finished bracelet. It was pretty and he was pleased with the way it had turned out. "I never made one like that before for anyone," he said. "But I always wanted to."

I pushed the mike aside and reached for the bracelet. "I like it," I said.

"Try it on. If it fits, I'll solder it."

I noticed the loose wire ends. "You mean I won't be able to get it off?" I pulled my hand back.

"You won't be able to if I solder it."

I thought what Dad and Mother would say if I walked in wearing a bracelet from Peter that I couldn't get off — if I wore it all summer.

"I can't wear it," I said. My voice sounded

near tears. The miserable feeling came rushing back.

They would say it meant a lot of stuff it
didn't; when it was just a yellow bracelet to
cheer me up.

"Something's real wrong," said Peter. He
was watching my face.

"Just my s-stupid parents," I said, struggling to be offhand, to get him away from the
subject. "You know how p-parents are." I
couldn't say any more.

"Big row?" I never heard so much sympathy in two tiny growly words.

I nodded. I wished he'd stop talking about
it and yet I hoped he wouldn't.

"Tell me what about?"

"I ca-an't."

"Tell me."

I hung my head and covered my face with
my hands. The room was hot and sticky. There
were no words for me to answer with.

I didn't move or say anything.

"They don't like you down here in the
basement. With me. Isn't that it? And they
told you why? All the gory details?"

I nodded.

"All right!" he shouted. "I'll tell you what!
We'll set up the blank-blank radio in the living room! We'll invite all four of them to sit
around and watch us! I hope they get some
real big thrills!

"Put down your paper, Dad!" he yelled.
"Don't take your eyes off us! We might do
something we'll regret the rest of our lives!"

He picked up an old radio tube and winged

it at the basement wall. It smashed and the broken pieces scattered across the floor. Spike barked and jumped and yapped with excitement.

"Damn them!" said Peter, hoarsely, staring at the mess.

"Peter!" I said. I had never seen him that way before.

"I'm sorry, Jo," he said, trying to get control. "But one minute they treat us as though we're in the sandbox. The next minute they scold about going steady. I wouldn't ever —" He looked at me and broke off. "They don't give us credit for any sense at all," he finished lamely.

All the mad had gone out of him. He sat down on the bench.

The upset had gone out of me, too, now that I didn't have to explain what was wrong. I gathered up Spike and climbed onto the table with him and hugged him. It was even exciting to have Peter get so mad on account of me. I squeezed Spike harder and wondered what would happen next.

Peter laughed, but not as though anything was too funny.

"You know . . . my father said, 'I don't like them spending all that time down in the basement if they aren't going steady'; and my mother said, 'I don't like them spending all that time down in the basement if they *are* going steady.'"

"Mine are worse," I said, and I told him the idiot business about me knowing his dog too well.

"Are you going steady with my dog?" said Peter, shaking his finger at me and Spike (who was trying to lick my cheek). "I won't tolerate that sort of behavior, young lady!"

"As long as we're paying the bills, young man —" I threatened.

"As long as you're under my roof, missy —"

"No son of mine —" I said. "I'll lock him up first —"

"How'd you know they said that?" asked Peter, astonished.

It was strange. I didn't mind at all talking to Peter about the fearful subject of going steady. Because we saw things the same way, *not* the way our parents saw them. Seeing things the way Peter did made it seem natural and happy and reassuring and funny.

"Anyway," I said, conversationally, swinging my legs back and forth under the table, "I hate the words 'going steady.' They sound grubby and common. Like chewing gum all the time, or wearing curlers downtown. Don't you think? I'm never going steady with anyone," I chattered on, rocking Spike back and forth in my lap.

But Peter was staring at me, as though he wasn't seeing me the usual way.

He made me blush.

"Well . . . you could say . . . something . . . maybe —" He was having trouble getting the words the way he wanted them (and Peter was wonderful with words). "You could say . . . like — two people might agree that they were . . . going to everything together?" He kept very busy with the pliers, but his voice had ended in a question and I knew that I was supposed to answer.

I stopped swinging my feet and let Spike jump down.

"Going to al-most everything together," I said. It was hard to know what might come up. I picked up the bracelet and twiddled with it.

"Going to al-most everything, together — for a while," Peter added, thoughtfully.

I remembered Mother talking about getting upset when attachments ended.

"That's terrible!" I said.

"Hemingway says *every* . . . *you* know ends in tragedy if it's continued long enough," said Peter, cheerfully.

The "*you* know" part was "love affair." Our English teacher talked about it once. Peter was a big Hemingway fan. I didn't like Hemingway much, but he was right about a lot of things. I knew he was right about love affairs ending in tragedy, and sometimes you didn't have to continue them very long at all.

I slid the bracelet on.

"What are you going to tell 'em?" asked Peter, his eyes bright with clinical interest.

"I am going to make the very solemn announcement," I said, putting on an owly face, "that Josephine Ann Frost and Peter Kevin Stern have agreed that they will be going to almost everything together and I don't care who knows it."

"For a while," said Peter.

"Cautious!" I accused. "Go ahead. Bust it up any time you want! I'll bear it bravely!" I was getting bubbly and giggly.

"A man doesn't like too many strings," said Peter, with dignity. "I'll solder the two ends together," he said, plugging in the iron.

While the iron heated I thought about how there was going to be a big blowoff when I got home and Dad said, "Where'd you get that thing on your wrist?" and Mother said, "Take it off," and I said, "I can't; it's soldered on." And I hoped I'd be able to hold my tongue while they argued and not sass them back with, "If you two don't like it you can lump it because it's one hundred per cent you two that got me into it. Peter and I would never have thought of such a thing all by ourselves."

But I knew we would have, sooner or later.

I sat down on the piano bench, feeling terribly grown up. "Hurry up and solder it," I said to Peter. "We're missing a lot of messages."

Peter looked at the transmitter. His eyes opened wide. He started to chuckle. He threw back his head and guffawed. "It's good you don't care who knows about it and all that," he said, with a wicked grin. He reached forward and did something to the mike.

"Why?"

"You left the mike on. We've been broadcasting. Every ham in Westchester County plus hundreds of walkie-talkies have heard us."

"Owwww!" I moaned.

"Buck up, old girl," he said, slapping me on the back. "I don't suppose your parents will have received more than five or six phone calls."

"Oh, Peter," I said. "What'll I do?"

"It will be all right." He left his hand on my shoulder. "Hemingway says —"

"I know," I said. "Hemingway says what you do is all right if you feel good about it afterward."

And I had the good feeling because I had an understanding with Peter that was comfortable and realistic for both of us.

Parents always worry because they think ahead of you; but usually they can be reasonable and can accept things when they understand your point of view. Mother could understand that the bracelet stood for a simple and uncomplicated bond between me and Peter. The bracelet meant that we could count on each other, and that we found joy and security, boy and girl, doing things together for a while. That was all.

Peter sat down beside me on the bench, "Hold still," he growled. "I don't want you to get burned."

I didn't think I would. I trusted him.

I watched him join the two ends of wire with a single drop of shining solder that shone clean and silver-bright a long, long time before it cooled and dulled.

8

She Was a Queen

All spring I had been looking forward to the shore as impatiently as ever, but when we were finally there nothing looked the same. I was restless and uncooperative with every member of the family, except for Grammy. So much seemed strange and different that I was more than grateful for Grammy. She was the only person I belonged with, the only solid link with summers past.

At times the days seemed doubly precious, as though they were in some way numbered; I was aware of flickers of nostalgia in advance, for my childhood summers at the shore. Other times I felt like bursting out, but out of what I couldn't figure.

Aunt Anne said, "Josie must be in love," but I hardly thought of Peter, except when his letters came or when someone asked me about the yellow bracelet.

I wanted to be left alone, but when I was alone I was lonesome. Mother was smart enough (and courteous enough) not to pry into my affairs, but she did ask me (along about the middle of July) if I'd like to invite Peter up for a week. "No, thank you," I said.

From a distance I had to admit that the thing I liked best about Peter was that he liked me. It is exciting and grown up to have someone feel that way about you and it made me fond of him. But the thought of having to amuse him for a week at the shore all by myself without any basketball games and movies and hamburger joints to go to was too dreary to contemplate.

I spent days dreading (out loud) Priscilla's return from France at the end of August. She had been in Paris all summer on a companion-tutoring deal that was recommended by the guidance counselor at school. I expected that, in my present frame of mind, we would do nothing but squabble.

Priscilla's plane landed at Kennedy Airport on a Wednesday, twelve days before Labor Day. Aunt Anne had planned in careful detail how Priscilla would take the limousine to New York, the local to Westchester, stay the rest of the week with Uncle Jack, and fly up with him on Friday evening.

Wednesday night about eleven o'clock Priscilla showed up at the shore. There was a frightful fracas. She told Aunt Anne that after her Air France plane had landed she hung around on standby until she caught a flight to Portland, Maine. From there she hopped a bus. She gave a little shrug of her left shoulder and said that it seemed simpler that way.

With all that luggage!

She stood under the porch light, deep tan

in her white sharkskin dress, while Aunt Anne kissed her and fussed and asked a steady stream of questions and tried frantically to get Uncle Jack on the phone.

I wasn't sure whether Aunt Anne noticed how thin she was or saw the dark circles under her eyes.

Before she went to bed she hung a few clothes in our closet. She said she was going to leave the rest of her things packed so I didn't need to move my stuff. Her voice was listless, faint, and faraway, as though nothing mattered to her at all — or ever would again.

If she had been a new person that I'd never met, I could have talked to her; but the way things had always been between us, if I'd said something kind or interested, she'd have thought I was being sarcastic or poking fun. So we hardly spoke except gently and politely about necessary things and we remained quiet and distant to each other for what remained of the summer.

And very little of the summer remained. We always left the shore right after Labor Day and those last few days turned out to be unexpectedly hectic.

Labor Day weekend started badly because Grammy's niece, Alison, and Alison's husband, Fred, and their two-year-old, Eric, suddenly invited themselves for the whole weekend at the very last minute.

Mother and Aunt Anne considered this a miserably irresponsible act. Friday evening, while we were sitting around the living room waiting for our guests, they ran through the Grievance List for the umpteenth time.

"It isn't as though they gave us any warning," Mother began. She had a pad of yellow paper in her lap and she was changing the amounts of food to buy.

"It was too late to get someone in to help out," said Aunt Anne.

"We'll all pitch in," said Grammy heartily. "I'm fond of Alison. Give me the list. Josie and I will do all the shopping and put everything away."

"I'd love it if you would," said Mother. "But you will try to stick to the list, won't you?" she asked anxiously.

"It means that Priscilla and Josephine have to give up their room and sleep in the tent," complained Aunt Anne. "All that switching around."

"I don't mind," I said.

"Mums is afraid I'll be propositioned by a porcupine," murmured Priscilla, sotto voce. Priscilla was developing some interesting possibilities.

"Why don't you relax —" Grammy started. But Aunt Anne cut in. "And then there's the matter of the child," she said.

"What's the matter with the child?" I asked in a flippant tone.

"Josie!" Mother exploded. "If you'd just take a realistic look at the work —"

"We'll do all the dishes," said Grammy, quickly, to prevent a scene between Mother and me. "Won't we, Josie?"

I nodded, but I wondered how much we'd really do. Grammy was good at campaign promises, but she was slippery as an eel when they tried to pin her down. Usually Mother and Aunt Anne accepted her failings with affectionate good humor, but their tempers were on the short side after a summer of it.

"That's what you always say," Aunt Anne was telling her, "and then you —"

"Please, please," said Dad. "The party's getting rough. What will our guests think?"

We managed to get along until Labor Day lunch without our guests thinking anything too awful, but by the end of that meal Aunt Anne and Mother were beginning to show signs of battle fatigue. Aunt Anne especially. She had produced a magnificent dinner of salmon and peas because, she said, "It's traditional in New England for Labor Day." Whereupon Uncle Jack had the bad taste (if you want to put it that way) to tell her that it was traditional for the Fourth of July, and Aunt Anne remembered that Uncle Jack was right. If I'd been Aunt Anne I'd have thrown it at him. After she'd shelled that mountain of peas! (Grammy had decided at the store that fresh peas would be tastier than the frozen ones that Mother had on the list.)

The air was thick with tension; I'd had enough. All I could think of was to get out of the house and away to the water. Peter would have said, *"Carpe diem* — seize the day."

Grammy had the same idea. "I believe I'll go for a little sail," she said, getting to her feet, "if the sloop isn't spoken for —"

Mother and Aunt Anne sighed in unison. Mother turned wearily to Alison. "We've been trying all summer to persuade Grammy that it isn't safe for her to sail," she said. "We just can't let her. Suppose you tipped over?" she asked Grammy.

"I'd bob around like a cork," said Grammy.

"Besides," said Aunt Anne, "it isn't appropriate. At your age!"

"Mums thinks it isn't . . . *comme il faut*," said Priscilla, with the little shrug of her left shoulder.

Pooh to all of them, I thought. Mother and Aunt Anne and Priscilla had this cooking and baking image that they were always trying to squeeze Grammy into. Sailing didn't fit.

Grammy opened her mouth to argue.

"I do think our guests might enjoy the sailboat," said Mother, looking archly at Grammy.

Grammy couldn't argue with that. She sat down again. "Well," she said, "I guess I'll —"

Mother put her fingers underneath her dessert plate and wobbled it up and down meaningfully. Dishes.

I held my breath. We'd done quite a few.

Grammy shook her head. I felt a chuckle inside. Tit for tat.

But there was a sneak attack from another quarter. "I know Grammy won't mind watching Eric," Aunt Anne was saying to Alison. "Of course he's too young for the sailboat."

What do you know! Child Care fitted the Senior Citizen image perfectly.

Grammy scowled. She was in a box. She couldn't say anything without offending Alison.

Alison and Fred left for the beach. Dad

went with them — "to show them the ropes," Aunt Anne said. She laughed at her little joke. Mother thought it was hilarious too.

Precious bright afternoon minutes ticked away and we were only halfway through the agony of the demitasse. Didn't they know we had this day only once?

Grammy pushed her chair back. "I'm going to put Eric in the rowboat and pull him around in the shallows between the mudflats," she announced, as she left.

"Oh, I don't know —" said Mother.

"No, no," said Aunt Anne. "She can't have the rowboat. I asked the boys to sail over in their Sailfish for some water skiing."

Not that, I thought. Anything but that.

She turned to Uncle Jack. "Jack?" she said. "Do you mind?"

Uncle Jack sighed. What he liked most was to lie in the hammock with a bottle of cold beer, a detective story, and a handkerchief over his bald head. But after his remark about the salmon he hadn't a prayer.

Priscilla (who had been wild about water skiing the summer before) had taken him to the boat show at the Coliseum in New York in January and had talked him into buying a gigantic outboard motor. When she came back from France she didn't give two hoots about water skiing any more. But Aunt Anne had to get some good out of the motor, so she kept inviting a pair of truly uninspiring boys to come and use it with us. Naturally they came. They couldn't help their hormones.

"Priscilla can ski first —"

Priscilla rose dutifully. I could tell that she

was going through the motions. She was doing well, too. If I hadn't been sharing a room with her, hadn't heard the muffled sobs, I'd have thought she was the same old Priscilla. I wished that I could talk to her.

"— and then Josie can have a turn."

"Oh, how nice," said Mother.

"I'd rather sit on the beach with Grammy," I said, to be difficult.

"Even better!" said Aunt Anne. "Someone to keep an eye on —" She raised her eyebrows at Mother.

"Yes, but this isn't an ideal combination," answered Mother. "They are as like as two peas."

"Two impossible peas," said Aunt Anne.

"*What* are you insinuating about me and Grammy?" I asked.

"I'm going to breathe a great sigh of relief when we get Grammy safely back to Westchester this year," said Mother.

"A-men!" said Aunt Anne.

"What could happen?" I asked. "We're going to sit on the beach. If the sloop gets back early we might take a little spin. That's all."

"Let's see if Grammy can forget about sailing for one afternoon," said Aunt Anne, sarcastically.

"Let's give it the old college try," said Mother.

"Sis boom bah!" I muttered to myself, watching them clear the table.

It took the better part of an hour to get Eric up and dressed in his little sunsuit and to find the pail and shovel and to fix a thermos of orange juice. The sun was making halfway shadows by the time we reached the bottom of the path with Eric toddling between us. I carried his sunhat and terrycloth wrapper. Grammy had the zwieback and the flask.

"Where shall we sit?" I asked.

Grammy didn't answer. She stood at the water's edge, looking across the so-familiar bay. Absorbing it. It soothed her, the way it soothed me, but I could tell she still had steam coming out her ears — from Aunt Anne's attitude about her.

"This is nice," I said, choosing a spot where the sand was powdery white and dry. I handed Eric the pail and shovel and walked down the beach to stand beside her.

Off to the right our sloop tacked off the mooring. I had left her rigged when I swam in for lunch, hours before. I watched the boom swing from port to starboard. The sun made a blinding dazzle on the white luffing sails and I could hear the creak and rattle of the rigging in the freshening breeze.

Joy made me fill my lungs with buoyant sea air; but suddenly the thought of the briefness of it brought almost-tears and I had to hang my head. We had only two more days. When there is so little time, I thought, they should let you do what you want to do.

As I watched the sunlit sparkles on the water, the sudden shadow of a cloud fell across it and put the glitter out. The water went somber gray.

"Grammy!" I called. I felt clammy, chill, startled to find her no longer beside me.

"Is that the Sailfish?" I heard her voice with

relief. She had walked a little way down the shore.

Breathing more easily, I looked where she pointed, past the concrete jetty. The diagonally striped white sail moved across the blue of the harbor like a child's painting. "Mmmmm," I answered.

"What are they like to sail?" she asked. "Tell me." She was making thoughtful designs in the sand with her toe.

I wanted to help her forget the way Mother and Aunt Anne made her feel so — extra. (So *de trop,* as Priscilla would say now that every other word was coming out French.)

To get Grammy's mind off it, even though I was sleepy, I told her about the Sailfish. "It's a bit like sailing a canoe," I said. "A Sailfish is a flat board, really. About thirteen feet long." I lay down on the hot sand and rested my head on my crossed arms. "Lateen rig," I mumbled. "They're fast and wet." It was easy to explain a boat to Grammy; she knew everything about them.

Pages of her scrapbooks came to mind. No matter what else happened, happy or sad, one thing was always the same. Every summer, pictures of Grammy sailing on the bay. Summer 1925: Old-fashioned brown and white photographs curled at the edges; Grandfather and Grammy in an amazing old catboat. Grammy told me once that she was a beamy old tub, but she could outrun anything in the harbor (as long as you didn't accidentally get her wrapped up in a North River jibe).

Summer 1928: Grammy in a borrowed

Starboat; sunsuited Aunt Anne (even at six, no sailor) waving from the jetty. Probably waiting for some little boy to paddle over to see her. Daddy was a year old then.

Summer 1933: The photographs were shiny black and white; Grammy in the sailing canoe with tiny Daddy (oh, those blond curls!) sitting amidships, wearing a sailor suit and a cork life preserver. He must have been too little to clamp the leeboards down; she was an expert sailor if she could take him out by herself. Behind them, along the path that summer, the trees were getting tall, halfway to full grown. That was the year that Grammy took flying lessons — until Grandfather found out about it. There was a picture of Grammy wearing her helmet and goggles and jump suit.

I had never known the real Grandfather, but I had him forever in the scrapbooks. My favorite picture is one of the first ones, right after they were married. Grandfather is standing tall, straight, proud, watching our very cottage being built on the high bluff. And beside him Grammy, so young, bright, hopeful, looking forward with him to the promise of endless summers, sailing, boys and girls to run up and down their path. The trees were young, then, along the path that descended to the beach. They were no taller than Grammy. Wild roses, pink-petaled, grew among the rocks. Sometimes when I was deep in that bright time that was finished —

"I don't suppose they're too tricky if you know how."

Grammy's voice broke into my reverie. I couldn't think what she was talking about.

Eric poured a bucketful of sand on my bare back. My skin shuddered.

I remembered the Sailfish. "They can be tricky when you first try," I said. I had tipped one over the summer before. "Oh, look at Uncle Jack!" I said to Eric, to keep him from pouring any more sand down the back of my bathing suit.

"Boat?" asked Eric.

Uncle Jack was staggering down the path with the gargantuan outboard. Priscilla walked ahead of him with the water skis.

"That's right," I told Eric. "The motor makes the boat go. Brrrm. Brrrm." He was getting pink, so I pulled the terrycloth wrapper around him.

"You're so good with children," said Priscilla, when she reached the sand where we were sitting. "Mums even says so." She paused beside us so that Uncle Jack could catch up.

Priscilla had spoken to me nicely. She even seemed somehow wistful about Eric. I decided she was not trying to make me feel silly. Nevertheless I couldn't seem to answer her. Eric and I had some orange juice without offering her any. Grammy passed out the zwieback.

I noticed that Grammy kept watching the Sailfish. It was standing off our point.

"Oh! Oh!" I said, hamming it up, rolling my eyes so that only the whites showed, the way Paul does sometimes. "Thrill! Thrill!" I said so loud that Priscilla jumped. "Here come the boys!" I felt horrible as soon as I said it.

Grammy chuckled, but she was the only one.

Priscilla stared. "What's got into you,

Jose?" she asked, with a puzzled frown.

She'd been so different since she'd been abroad; the nastiness was all me. I didn't know how to shake myself out of the old pattern. Priscilla left us and went on to the jetty, and I couldn't blame her.

As she left, Uncle Jack thumped up to us. "Great God," he said, resting the motor beside Grammy. "Thing weighs a holy ton." He mopped his bald head with his handkerchief. "*You* look comfortable, Mother," he continued sociably, wiping the steam from his glasses.

"I don't know," said Grammy.

"Trade places," said Uncle Jack, genially kidding her. He took out a cigarette and fitted it into the holder.

"All right, Jack," said Grammy, getting to her feet with purpose. "You fasten the motor to the transom and show me how to start her up —"

"Oh, Mother!" said Uncle Jack. He looked around for help. He needed Aunt Anne. Poor Uncle Jack becomes unglued when he's up against more than one determined female at a time.

"Sure!" I said, getting to my feet also. "You can take care of Eric. Grammy and I —"

"No! No!" said Uncle Jack, backing away.

"Dad-dy!" Priscilla called, from the end of the jetty.

"Oh, my, my," said Uncle Jack, hugging the motor. I thought of a toad struggling with an enormous mushroom. I had to laugh. He frowned at me reproachfully and dragged it away.

I looked for Grammy to enjoy it with me, but she wasn't watching. She was frowning, smoothing the sand with the palm of her hand in huge restless semicircles. "I wish you'd go with Priscilla," she said. "You'd have more fun."

"I'd rather stay here with you," I said.

She scooped up a handful of sand and watched the grains slip through her fingers, slowly but relentlessly, as they run through the thin neck of an hourglass. " 'Grow old along with me,' " she said. " 'The best is yet to be,' In a pig's eye!"

The way she said it disturbed me. It gave me the same empty, bottomless-pit feeling that I sometimes get when the sun goes down in the late afternoon. I had a chilly premonition and I couldn't shake it.

"I never liked that one much anyway," I said, forcing it a little to make her feel better. "What I like is: 'The year's at the spring. The day's at the morn,'—" We were both Browning buffs.

"For *you*, Josie," Grammy said shortly.

"Come on, Grammy," I said. "Let's not ruin the afternoon because we couldn't sail today. There's always —" I thought about how much more important today must be when there weren't so many tomorrows and I felt goose pimples rising on my legs.

I understood my mood. I was feeling bad because it was September of the year (and — I began to see — the September of my childhood), but it was the September of Grammy's whole life. I rubbed my legs hard, as if getting rid of the bumps would get rid of the mood.

"Don't worry, Josie," she said, in her everyday warm, reassuring voice. "You know, old age itself doesn't bother me. But please help me never to see myself as others evidently see me. Better one gay 'today' than an endless succession of dismal tomorrows!" She was looking at Uncle Jack on the jetty as she spoke.

"I'll always see you as you really are," I said, glad she was cheering up.

The Sailfish, with its gay red sail, was pulling alongside the jetty.

"I expect I'll still have a chance to sail," she mused contentedly.

"Absolutely!" I answered. "That's the spirit!" But it was hard to see how, because the sloop was way offshore.

"Boat?" asked Eric. He started to totter rapidly toward the jetty and the Sailfish.

"Hey!" I said. "Come back!" I scrambled to my feet.

"Let's all go look," said Grammy. "Tell me. Does it have a centerboard or leeboards?" she asked as we made our barefoot way across the burning sand.

"Daggerboard," I said, holding tight to Eric's chubby hand. "It's the same as a centerboard, really."

One of the boys had gotten into the rowboat (at the sloop mooring, where Dad had left it) and was sculling it in. The other boy was standing on the jetty, holding the Sailfish by the mast.

"Hey, Josie," called the boy on the jetty.

"Get me a piece of line, will you? I want to make fast to the jetty."

"I'll have to go all the way up to the house," I objected.

"Go ahead," said Grammy. "I'll watch Eric." She practically pushed me.

I detached his little hot hand and turned him over to Grammy.

I had to root around all over the musty, spidery basement, but finally I found some spare clothesline. I could hear Aunt Anne and Mother overhead, finished with the dishes, getting ready for a quiet bit of beach. I stopped upstairs for a banana and then started back down the path with the rope.

It was bright outside and I had to squint. I heard the sudden roar of the outboard motor and, with my hand shading my eyes, I saw the rowboat peel away from the jetty. Uncle Jack and both boys were in the power rowboat, towing Priscilla on skis.

Aunt Anne never liked Priscilla to get her hair wet, so Priscilla had learned to go off the jetty half standing up. I had to admire the way she did it.

It made me cross that the boys had sent me all the way up to the house for nothing and I wondered how they had managed to make the Sailfish fast without the line. From halfway down the sloping path I could see only the triangular tip of the sail sticking up on the far side of the jetty. Eric was standing right on the edge of the jetty looking down in the deep water where the Sailfish floated. Grammy was nowhere to be seen.

"Hey!" I shouted, starting to run. "WATCH

OUT! GET BACK! It's too deep!" Eric turned calmly to look at me. "DON'T MOVE!" I yelled.

Why had she left him?

I tore down the path and across the sand and onto the jetty.

When I stood beside him, I asked, "Where's Grammy?" in as normal a voice as I could muster, so as not to scare him.

He pointed down. "Boat," he said.

Grammy was sitting on the Sailfish, dangling her bare legs in the water, fending the boat off the concrete walls of the jetty. Her cotton dress trailed in the water and her face was all soft happy smiles.

"One of Priscilla's friends," said Grammy, kicking one leg up and down, watching the bright droplets. "I told him I'd hold his boat."

"Love-ly," I said. It was a grand place to sit, lifting and falling on the slight sea, listening to the lap-slapping of the wavelets against the wooden hull. I lay on my stomach on the sun-warm, shell-pocked concrete to make the line fast to the mast. Eric copied me, giggling, his little squirmy body lying close. We plopped concrete pebbles into the water.

A shout from the house made us all jump. "Mother!" shouted Aunt Anne. She was hanging out an upstairs window. From that height she had an unobstructed view of Grammy sitting on the boat. "Get right off that boat at once!" commanded Aunt Anne.

"You must be in mortal danger down there," I said to Grammy. "Pardon me for not noticing."

"Doesn't take much to get Anne unstrung,"

said Grammy. "Especially where boats are concerned."

I went on fastening the rope.

The screen door whanged and Mother shot out onto the porch.

"Hang onto the boat, Josie," she called. "We'll help you get her off."

"It's contagious," I said.

The door banged again. Aunt Anne was on Mother's heels. She didn't seem too well done up.

To see their excitement you'd have thought Grammy was going down for the third time, not just taking the air on a tied-up boat. They started running down the path, doing up buttons as they ran.

Grammy looked a bit anxious. "They're coming into the stretch," she said.

Aunt Anne was on the beach. "Why can't you . . . sit on the porch . . ." she panted, ". . . like other women . . ." (puff puff) ". . . your age . . ." She had big, deep frown lines. "You're much too old —"

"Josie?" said Grammy, suddenly, sharply, shortly. She had shifted to a businesslike position in the stern of the Sailfish; she held the sheet and the tiller correctly.

She took me by surprise.

If I'd said, "No, Grammy, you shouldn't," she wouldn't have done it, but you don't usually think in terms of telling your grandmother she shouldn't do things. At least, I didn't then.

"I want to fall off on the starboard tack," she said.

"All right," I answered. "Back the main until you clear the end of the jetty." I reached for her glasses. With my other hand I held the bow off, to catch the wind. "Ready?" I asked.

Grammy trimmed the sail hard amidships. "Shove off!" she ordered.

"Go!" I answered.

"Josie pushed her," said Aunt Anne accusingly.

"What did you do that for?" asked Mother.

The wind caught the tight sail and the boat gave a sudden lurch and heeled sharply. Grammy yelped and slid sideways.

"Are you all right?" I called.

There were banshee wails from the Greek chorus on the jetty.

Grammy scrambled up to windward.

"Fall off!" I shouted.

"No. No. Stay on the boat," shouted Aunt Anne.

"Fall off the wind," I said, witheringly, "not the boat."

Skillfully paying out sheet, Grammy scudded into the bay.

"Swim after her!" said Aunt Anne, hypnotized by the flat hull streaking away from us.

Who could catch a planing Sailfish? Grammy settled herself comfortably with her wet skirt pulled up about her. I saw that her muscles remembered from when she sailed the canoe. I knew how she was feeling the fresh summer wind on her cheeks and the sting of drying salt water on her legs. And most of all, the joy of racing across the sparkling water, heeled over, running the lee rail under.

I saw her shake out her long hair into the same breeze that lifted my hair and cooled the back of my neck. She was singing a thin reedy song of timelessness and freedom, of a gloriously gay "today."

To Aunt Anne and Mother it must have sounded like a cry for help.

"The canoe!" said Aunt Anne. She clambered off the jetty onto the beach. Mother and Eric toddled along behind.

Aunt Anne picked up the bow of the canoe and Mother picked up the stern so that all the water in Mother's end rushed down to Aunt Anne's end and naturally Aunt Anne dropped it.

Neither one of them has a scrap of a sense of humor about boats. They started to argue. They had another go at it with the same results. Slop. Slurp. Drop.

It was bad for the canoe so I laid Grammy's glasses on the jetty and went to help. By the time I got there they had dragged it to the water and Aunt Anne was sitting in the bow seat. I took a quick look around for Grammy and decided that I'd better hop into the stern seat instead of Mother.

As a rescue party Mother and Aunt Anne were considerably less than useless. I didn't want to spoil Grammy's fun, but she had me worried. She was still sailing straight out into the bay. The outboard-rowboat was well off to the right, out of hailing distance. Grammy should have tacked back. It wasn't sensible. She hadn't soloed in years, and never on a Sailfish. They could be tricky. I had thought (if I thought at all) that she was just planning to fool around near the end of the jetty. She should have had more sense at her age.

I jumped into the stern seat and shoved off in one smooth motion so that the canoe shot out into the bay before Aunt Anne could turn her head. "Take care of Eric," I called back to Mother.

"Josie!" exclaimed Aunt Anne. "What are you going to do?"

I saw, with relief, that Grammy had tacked and was heading for the jetty, so I decided to tool around in innocent circles (But look, Aunt Anne, I'm paddling as hard as I can and we just go *round* and *round*) until Grammy had safely enjoyed as much sailing as she wanted.

I reckoned without the rowboat and its powerful outboard. From his position off to the right, Uncle Jack must have seen the Sailfish leave the jetty. He changed course, with Priscilla still in tow, to buzz the Sailfish (with *me* sailing it, I suppose he thought). I put on steam and headed the canoe toward the action, fast, with Aunt Anne squealing, "Don't tip! Don't tip!" and clutching the gunwales for dear life.

We caught up with the Sailfish about fifty feet offshore at the same time that Uncle Jack and the boys intercepted her. When Uncle Jack saw Grammy at the helm, his face was a caution. "Mother!" he gasped, as Grammy shot by him on her way back to the jetty. He cut his motor abruptly, reducing speed so that Priscilla began to submerge.

"No. No," shouted Aunt Anne, standing up in the canoe. "Priscilla's hair!"

Later Aunt Anne insisted to Mother that I made the canoe lurch on purpose. At any rate, it tipped wildly and Aunt Anne fell in with a splash a few feet from Priscilla. Relieved of Aunt Anne's weight, the canoe righted itself, leaving me sitting in the stern seat.

Priscilla struggled bravely to keep her hair above the water. She would have succeeded, too, had not Uncle Jack (trying, always trying, to accommodate his women) chosen this moment to become unglued again. Not thinking, he restarted the motor and Priscilla, still holding the towrope, was jerked unexpectedly down and under.

Her skis came off her feet and shot up out of water, right beside Aunt Anne, like two porpoises jumping for food. Aunt Anne shrieked and grappled for the side of the canoe, which naturally tipped and took some water before I was able to balance her weight with mine and right it again.

I was doubled up laughing until I noticed that Grammy (whom I had expected, by that time, to be safely tied up at the jetty) had, instead, tacked again and was headed straight for the shambles of boats, ski ropes, and swimmers.

"Go back to shore!" I warned between cupped hands. "Stay away from this mess!"

But she held her course for us and gleefully maneuvered between the boats, cleverly avoiding the clutching hands of the boys in the power rowboat. She hadn't counted on Aunt Anne and Priscilla in the water, dead ahead. She was forced to tack again, unexpectedly. The daggerboard, hanging like a keel two feet below the Sailfish in the water, snagged on the trailing ski rope. The Sailfish jerked to an abrupt halt, tipped, and dumped Grammy in to join the family circle.

It all happened so fast. Up to that moment it was like watching a slapstick comedy, but when I heard Grammy cry out as she hit the shocking, cold water, I got scared. Her head went under.

"Grammy!" I called, watching the place where she went down. I leaned as far over as I could from the half-swamped boat, but I couldn't reach.

"Uncle Jack!" I shouted, in panic.

Grammy fought to get her head up, but her wet clothes were a drag. I slid into the water beside her. One of the boys cut the motor and held out an oar.

"All right," Grammy gasped, struggling to tread water. She even tried to laugh at the sight of her skirt, air-ballooned about her.

"Be quiet!" I ordered. "Save your breath!"

She looked stunned, to be so addressed by me.

Uncle Jack, short of wind, panting, helped me to get Grammy (and Priscilla and Aunt Anne) into the power rowboat.

Stiffly and without speaking the boys righted their Sailfish and set sail for home. The sun was low and the wet sail was dark, dark red.

"A dip in the salt water makes one feel zesty, huh, Jack?" said Grammy, heartily, cheerfully, recovered. "You should have a swim too." She nudged him with her elbow.

Uncle Jack didn't answer.

"Mother. Your skirt," said Aunt Anne firmly.

Grammy pulled it way down over her knees and looked around uneasily.

Uncle Jack had the outboard throttled way down and I swam easily alongside, pushing the canoe ahead of me, but no one would look at me or speak to me. I thought about how I could have said, "No, Grammy, you'd better not," and she wouldn't have.

Mother was waiting at the end of the jetty, holding Grammy's glasses.

"Grammy's hair," said Eric, soberly pointing. Grammy's hair hung in gray strings to her waist.

"We'll have to get Grammy right up to the house and into some nice dry clothes, won't we?" said Mother in the exasperated tone that she uses for small, naughty children.

"Don't act like that!" I said. "As if Grammy was old and gaga!"

"I'll get around to you in a little while, young lady," said Mother in a voice that made my knees weak. "There are quite a few things that you don't seem to understand."

All summer I hadn't been wanting to understand.

Grammy was starting to shiver, not from cold, but from Mother and everyone being so mad. They almost never got mad at her, but they had a right to be mad and Grammy knew it. She had no right to exasperate everyone and frighten them and make more work for them.

Priscilla paused beside me with the skis. She looked at me as though she couldn't possibly understand anyone acting the way I had, and then went up the path without a word.

Aunt Anne was assisting Mother with Grammy, scolding like a bluejay. I said to her in a forced little voice, "Grammy can walk by herself."

"Out of my way," snapped Aunt Anne. "You take after her. You're just as impossible as she is. You've gone too far this time." She had her most scowling face.

Grammy's scrapbook pages fluttered to mind: Aunt Anne's baby picture that gave Grammy so much joy, that cheerful smiling baby. What had happened while Aunt Anne grew up? Had flighty, irresponsible Grammy forced Aunt Anne to be a nervous, too-responsible child? Grammy had failed Aunt Anne somewhere along the line and they both knew it.

I didn't sass Aunt Anne back. Instead I stood aside and let her pass; I stayed behind, standing at the bottom of the path. Uncle Jack struggled past me with the outboard motor (an ant with a bread crumb) up the path between the full-grown, drooping trees.

The petals of the roses had blown away, leaving only the hard knobs of the rose apples which contained the seeds of a new generation. I thought of Grammy at the house (which Grandfather built for her, when she was a queen). Being picked at for worrying them. Being chivvied into doing up her hair. Being fussed at and scolded into a clean cotton dress and maybe an apron.

Sun-going-down emptiness ballooned inside me, and even if I didn't want to I had to think the other thought, the awful black thought that something had almost happened to Grammy and if we weren't careful it was certain to. It might not matter to Grammy how many tomorrows there were (as long as she enjoyed today), but it mattered to me too much. As far as I was concerned it was another right she didn't have, the right to be prodigal with her very self.

And then I knew that I was going to join the ranks of pickers and chivviers and fussers and scolders. Because it had to be that way, as they had understood for a long time and I hadn't. But I hoped that I could go about it so that Grammy would always see herself the way she wanted to, not the way the rest of us saw her.

The ebbing tide washed the jetty softly. Overhead, gray clouds were touched with sunset rose beneath. The waves had flattened under the falling breeze almost to pink-streaked glass. Away offshore the sloop's sails hung lifeless against the mast. Another summer was almost over. I could hardly bear the level sea, and the silence, and the salt taste, and I wanted to run, stumbling, up the hill, looking to Grammy for comfort as I had done all my life before.

But instead I walked up the path slowly, and around behind the house under the oak tree and in the back door.

I found Aunt Anne and Mother in the kitchen as I expected. They stopped talking so I knew they had been discussing me.

"I'm very sorry," I said.

"That's all right," said Mother.

"We don't think it was really your fault," said Aunt Anne.

I wondered if Aunt Anne thought it was at all *her* fault, for calling Grammy too old. Or if Grammy thought it was *her* fault, for making Aunt Anne into the kind of person she was. Fault is a meaningless word when you try to use it about other people. I thought, because you never know the whole story. Only about yourself do you know the whole story. The only person you can fault fairly is yourself.

There was no sound except the knife against the cutting board. Mother went on slicing Uncle Jack's home-grown tomatoes.

"Go ahead," I said. "I'm ready to talk about it."

"There are some things we are going to have to insist on," said Aunt Anne. "For her protection."

"She thinks you . . . admire her behavior," said Mother, carefully, without looking at me. "You provide . . . a sort of last link with the way she used to be when Grandfather was alive."

"She never got over Grandfather," said Aunt Anne.

"We aren't trying to spoil her fun," said Mother.

"Just help her put on the brakes," said Aunt Anne.

"You could help a lot," said Mother.

"She confides in you," said Aunt Anne.

"I get it," I said. My eyes stung, but I went on flippantly. "What you want is: Josephine Ann Frost, Girl Stool Pigeon."

"You don't need to put it quite that way," said Mother gently. "But we need you on our team."

My face must have shown that I wasn't too thrilled with the lineup.

"There's something else," said Aunt Anne, diffidently. "You've been a little . . . 'off' this summer, child. You've needed a friend your own age. Another girl. I've sometimes thought that Grammy has been trying to fill the gap for you."

Day after summer day came to mind. My eyes flooded. I felt like a boat suddenly cut adrift from its last mooring.

"Mea culpa!" I said in a stagey voice, to accept my blame lightly, to hide my feelings. *"Mea maxima culpa!"*

"What's that she says?" Aunt Anne asked Mother as I went through the swinging door.

"She gets it from Peter. You know how he likes Latin," Mother explained. "She uses it when she's upset. She says it's all her fault. Her very great fault."

"Poor child," said Aunt Anne.

In the living room Grammy was sitting by the front window watching the sun go down over her bay. She wore a clean, rose-petaled print. They hadn't talked her into an apron and the corners of her mouth turned up.

"That looks better!" I said, a little too cheerfully. I felt awkward because I had been talking about her behind her back.

"Mmmm," she said, trying to read my face. "What's doing this evening? Can't we stir up something? Maybe Alison and Fred —"

"Couldn't say," I answered, faking a yawn. "But you'll have to count me out. I'm turning in early."

She looked at me suspiciously.

"Yup," I said. "I must be getting old. I can't keep up with you these days."

"No stamina," she chuckled, still watching me closely. "Your generation has no stamina."

"Well, when they made you they broke the mold," I said saucily. "Everyone knows that."

She looked at me over the top rims of her glasses. "But they kept a big hunk of the same clay for you, young lady. Don't you forget that. No matter what they tell you." She tossed her head toward the kitchen door.

"As it happens I had figured that out," I said, looking at her over the top rims of my nonexistent glasses. "Because we have the same flaws. And that's why I've been elected a Committee of One."

"Is that what they told you?" Her eyes, warm brown, like mine, sparkled with life. "Are you your Grandmother's Keeper?"

I wanted to say, "Yes, I am. Because I want to keep you around as long as possible."

But instead, I told her, "Because you are older than I am, and you know me so well —" (I flashed her a demure and winning smile) "I'm supposed to see that *you* set *me* a good example. I've been such a prob-lem to everyone this summer," I said rolling my eyes.

"I see," she said. "In other words they'd like *me* to keep *you* out of trouble this evening by staying home with you and playing double solitare." (No one had fooled her a bit.)

"That's the sort of thing they have in mind," I said. (Least of all me.)

Her cheeks flushed healthy rose in anticipation; she loved a fast card game.

"Your deal," she said, getting out the cards. "But don't let either one of us forget that I'd as soon suddenly drop dead as spend the next twenty years doing the Senior Citizen bit on the front porch in a rocking chair, the way Anne would like me to." She smiled her secret, inward, indomitable, rascally smile. There were no barriers between us and I felt entirely at ease.

Grammy had her wish. A week before Halloween, on a beautiful red-gold autumn Saturday, with the bluest sky imaginable.

I had planned to have dinner with her and spend the night, and I was packing a bag and deciding which schoolbooks to take, when the phone rang. Grammy had gone downtown shopping. She had a stroke at the bakery. She must have been buying a coconut cake. I knew what had happened immediately from the way Mother looked at me.

I made a terrible scene Halloween evening because I thought it was shameful and unfeeling to allow Paul to go out Trick or Treating. I screamed at Mother and Daddy, "Nobody in this whole house ever cared a thing about Grammy except for me!"

Daddy looked at me quietly, as though he was trying to straighten out something for himself. "Some of us have more to remember than others," he said. "It's hard now . . . but you'll be glad, later."

It was too soon for me to understand.

November was cruelly beautiful. With crisp, cold, star-studded nights and day after day of bare twigs laced against the same mocking blue. There was no wind that month. Just the awful stillness; like the vapor trail after a jet has gone by, or the afterglow of a sunset across a frozen winter lake, or a forlorn and empty guest room after a special and honored guest has suddenly been called home.

9

Christmas Gifts

Thanksgiving was hard. I couldn't forget the year before when Grammy had come up to admire my newly painted room. But I knew, as well as I knew my own name, that I had to keep going. I did, and after the snow came, like a warm fluffy blanket, I began to feel better.

By the beginning of December I understood that every member of the family missed Grammy dreadfully, each in his own way and for his own memories. And as it became easier to talk about her again, I knew that she would not be forgotten. I was surprised to find that Mother, who was occasionally cross with her, missed her especially.

I was learning not to judge relationships between grown-ups until I had looked at them pretty carefully and from everybody's point of view. I only wished that they would show me the same courtesy and not keep jumping to erroneous conclusions. Because I was having a bit of a relationship problem myself.

And with Christmas just around the corner my problem was getting worse every minute.

If there were only some way that you could look up in a book what to get someone and then go out and buy it and hand it over and be done with it.

Gifts were too complicated. Sometimes the gift itself, the actual object, was everything. Other times the object couldn't matter less, it was all the thought and the intention behind it.

For instance, if Paul gave me a copy of Elizabeth Barrett Browning's sonnets for Christmas I'd love the book, but the thought wouldn't be anything because I'd know Mother bought it and said, "Here, wrap this up and give it to Josie."

If Mother and Dad gave me the book the thought would mean more, because they understood how I like the poems (especially "How Do I Love Thee?") and they cared enough to give me what I really wanted.

If Peter gave me Elizabeth Barrett Browning's love sonnets it would mean — oh, dear. I hoped he wouldn't!

I couldn't seem to talk to anyone about it and by the time Christmas was only three days away I had worked myself into a lather.

Mother got me up early that morning and made me get dressed and eat breakfast. When I was finished she pulled me into the living room and told me I had to help her put up Christmas decorations. I sat on the sofa and stared at the cardboard boxes.

"Josie," said Mother, when she couldn't contain herself any longer. "Try putting some of that balsam on the mantel. Hang those red and silver balls on it. Pull yourself together, for heaven's sakes!"

I could hear the irritation in her voice. I was a clod, a drag. But putting up Christmas decorations was bringing Christmas that much closer.

"I don't like to keep at you," said Mother, pushing a fake wreath at me, "but I am really anxious to finish this room before Anne and Priscilla show up." She was getting cross. I had forgotten they were coming over before lunch to make plans for New Year's weekend.

I hooked the wreath over the window latch and flopped a piece of balsam onto the mantel and stuck a red ball into it.

I had worried and slaved through the last week of school to get all my work in on time and the thing that kept me going was the thought of two glorious weeks to collapse and do as I pleased. Mostly read. But since vacation had started all I'd heard was: get up; do the decorations; write your cards; plan with Priscilla.

And worst of all I'd been putting off buying Peter's present until vacation and it was already Thursday and Christmas was Saturday.

"I'd rather be back in school," I said out loud, letting the balsam slide every which way.

Mother blew. "Sit down on that sofa, young lady," she said. "You and I are going to have a little talk."

I sat down and hardened up my face.

"I simply fail to understand you," she said. "You have absolutely everything. Christmas.

An attractive, reliable young man to take you around to all the vacation doings —"

Mother had changed about Peter. She found my situation most convenient. She never had a moment's worry when I was with Peter. And why should she?

I twisted the yellow Turk's Head on my wrist.

"You have to learn to give more of yourself to people," Mother was droning on. "Giving can be a privilege. It isn't often that the opportunity comes along to do something important for someone —"

"So I'll put up the balsam," I said.

"You have a lot to offer, Josie. Don't you know that it's more blessed to —"

"Mother, please!" I said. "Spare me!"

I went on picking at the bracelet. The yellow insulation had chipped in places and the solder joint had lost its luster. Two of the three strands had sprung loose and the third was about to go.

"Maybe he'll give you something . . . more permanent for Christmas," said Mother kindly. "Then you can get rid of that old thing. Is that what's bothering you?"

It was, but not the way she thought.

"Have you anything for him?" she asked.

I thought how with Peter and me the objects weren't important, the idea was everything.

"Something in leather for his desk?" asked Mother.

And how it wasn't often that you were in the position that your gift was the most important thing about Christmas to someone.

"A book?" asked Mother.

And how I was in that position with Peter. The doorbell rang.

Whatever I gave him would stand for the relationship between us and would affect the future.

"Whatever you decide on you'd better get this afternoon," said Mother.

I wanted to hide my head under the sofa pillows, but I stood up and spoke agreeably to Aunt Anne and Priscilla as they entered the living room.

Priscilla was wearing one of the shifts that had become her trademark. I hadn't seen much of Priscilla after those two brief weeks in September at the shore. The few times we'd been together we'd been almost shy. I did hear around school that her trip to Paris was a great success. No one knew if the French kid learned English, but Priscilla came back speaking flawless French.

Evidently she hadn't had quite as much supervision as Aunt Anne had been led to expect. After Dad had seen her several times during the fall, he said, "One of these days Anne is going to meet her match."

"What do you mean?" I asked.

"Priscilla has been pretty much under Anne's thumb," he said. "She's very immature —"

"We must be thinking of different Priscillas," I said. "She's been going out with boys since — always."

"Different parts of people mature at different rates," said Dad. "Your relationship with Mother is much more grown-up."

It was. Mother picked on me about little things, like Peter's present, because she didn't want to get stuck with driving me downtown at the last minute; but she let me decide the big ones for myself. Whereas Aunt Anne —

Aunt Anne was fingering the balsam and telling Mother where she could get some that was fresher for less. She had a calendar under one arm, to work out dates. Mother said she had something big up her sleeve to tell us about.

"Let's get going, Mums," said Priscilla.

She was standing with one elbow on the mantel. It was strange how she had slimmed down and I had filled out until we were about the same size.

I tried to look at her dress without seeming to notice it, which wasn't easy, because she was wearing contact lenses and she didn't miss a thing any more. She started making the dresses when school began and she sold them around town (which scandalized Aunt Anne). But Priscilla didn't seem to care too much. She shrugged her little French shrug and said, "My dressmaking is Mumsy's *bête noire* this year," and went right on turning them out. Priscilla seemed to have learned a great deal in Paris and I wondered who had taught her.

The dress was a simple shift and could be worn sleeveless or over a black knit turtleneck. The gimmick was that Priscilla appliquéd a piece of pop art somewhere on the dress. When you ordered your "priscilla" you didn't get to say what you wanted or where it was to go. Priscilla sewed them on just *any-where*. It was brilliant. Like, one girl had a hamburger down near the hem in the back; another had a green snake crawling around her waist and up her front. No one knew whether Priscilla was kidding about her haute couture or deadly serious and everyone was very respectful. She'd had a kind of aura about her since she'd come back from France.

I had to admire her. When you got your dress everyone crowded around and said, "Ooooo — turn around. Isn't it lovely. Let's see what you got. Let's see where she put it." Priscilla's dresses were terribly "in."

I didn't have a "priscilla." I'd have given anything for one, but I'd have died sooner than ask her, because of the way we'd always been. We had disliked each other so intensely. Since September, though, I'd begun to wonder whether Mother and Aunt Anne had anything to do with the dislike that we had for each other. They never showed much, but you can't kid kids.

As a matter of fact it was pretty embarrassing not to have a shift, so I'd been going around saying, "I'd as soon come to school in a *burlap bag* as wear one of those sick, phony French things Priscilla makes."

"— cocoa after skating," Mother was saying, looking over Aunt Anne's shoulder at the calendar.

"Escorts are being a problem this season," said Aunt Anne.

I'd heard that Priscilla wasn't going out much, but I thought that maybe this year's crop of seniors was beneath her. I imagined when the college crowd was home on vacation she'd be having her usual whirl.

"What a comfort to have Josie settled," said Aunt Anne.

She meant Peter. And settled meant:

Every Friday night: Change clothes. Walk to the movies with Peter. Sit with Peter. Have a soda. Hear about dogs and Latin poetry. Walk home exactly on time.

Every Saturday afternoon: Change clothes. Walk to the football game with Peter. Sit with Peter. Don't look at anybody else. Hear about football players I have known. Walk home exactly in time for dinner.

Every Saturday night: Change clothes —

Thank heavens I wasn't allowed to go out school nights!

But there was no school for the next two weeks.

I'd worked so hard and I hadn't had a mark below a B (even math) and I deserved a rest — two weeks to do as I pleased, which was to go to my room and shut the door and pull up my green comforter and read Dumas. I was on *Twenty Years After*. D'Artagnan was all right, but Athos was for me and I couldn't wait. I didn't deserve a vacation full of headaches over Peter.

Peter and I had had a dreary argument the day school got out and it hadn't really been patched up. Peter had come to school that morning shattered. He had discovered in a history book that Dido and Aeneas had actually lived two hundred years apart in real life and couldn't possibly have known each other. He was working on Book Four of *The*

Aeneid, which is their love story. He had translated almost half of it into rhyming couplets in dactylic hexameter. It was to be his magnum opus. Finding the bad news in a history book was the worst possible thing, because he had always hated history.

When he told me, I said, "Peter, it doesn't really matter if they actually knew each other. Don't you see? Virgil putting them in the book together was more important than their whole real lives."

And Peter said, "Well, that's a crazy way to look at it." He'd been getting very critical of everything I thought, in recent weeks, especially if it was different from him.

So I said, "You have no imagination at all. Who'd remember a thing about them if they were just ordinary people?"

And Peter said, "I suppose you'd rather be in a book with some guy you never met, than . . . than —"

I answered him as meekly as possible, "No, Peter, of course not." But he wasn't sure, and neither was I.

"I really think *you* should tell them," Mother was saying.

"No, *you,*" said Aunt Anne.

I'd tried to tell Peter that I might not always feel like going out, but he was such a darn nice boy. (I guess that's what's called "damning with faint praise.") It was just that if he were to leave town permanently on Christmas morning it would solve all my problems. I'd probably be so relieved that I'd float up in the air like a balloon.

"Josie," said Mother. *"Please* pay attention.

Aunt Anne and Uncle Jack are giving you and Priscilla a little New Year's Eve party for a Christmas present."

"We thought about a hundred," said Aunt Anne, bridling and beaming.

I literally felt sick. Peter would be in seventh heaven at such a thing. And every person there, all one hundred of them, would ask us back — as a couple.

"Mother!" said Priscilla. "What's the big idea of announcing this without consulting me first?"

"Now, Sweet," said Aunt Anne, holding up her hands. "Dads and I are doing this to get you back in the swim. I mean —"

Fine, I thought. Gimme arsenic next time.

"Well," said Mother, forcing cheerfulness. "That's settled."

Not quite, I thought. I will speak to Mother about this later, in private.

"They really should pick out the invitations this afternoon," said Aunt Anne.

Priscilla switched her long blonde hair from side to side. She wore it straight, the way I used to. Slender jade earrings dangled from her pierced ears. I wished my ears were pierced, but I didn't know who I dared ask to do it. Priscilla's shift was tan, with a large emerald-green Dali watch on one hip. Aunt Anne eyed it uneasily from time to time.

I'd like to see Priscilla in the ring with Aunt Anne, I thought. She couldn't make it on her own, but she might if she had a pro in her corner.

"They could meet at the bookstore around four thirty," said Mother, avoiding my scowling face. "The one next to the jewelry store. Josie had some shopping to do, too."

"Josie can spend the night with us," said Aunt Anne. "They can work on the invitations together. All right, dear?" she asked me.

I was unable to be rude to Aunt Anne. "All right," I said.

"That will work out nicely with buying something for Peter," said Mother.

Pickety pick pick pick!

"All *right!*" I said, "All *right*. All *right*."

The door had hardly closed behind them before I said, "Mother, do I *have* to?"

She said, "No, Josie. I have already spoken to your father and we both feel that this is a little much. But we didn't think it fair to turn it down *for* you."

"Whew!" I said. "I'll call her this afternoon."

"I thought I'd call Anne and explain," said Mother quickly. "Don't you think that would be easier?"

"No," I said. "It was offered to me, so I'll tell her. I don't mind telling people things."

I could see that Mother was torn. She was pleased that I wanted to handle my own affairs, but she didn't want a family flap right before Christmas. Especially with Dad's family.

She didn't know that I'd never flap with Aunt Anne again, because Aunt Anne had been unexpectedly kind to me at the shore when I was so rude to her; and because she had stood by me at the Spring Get-Together when I was such a fool over Henry; and most of all, because she had never mentioned either incident to Mother.

Having people help you when you are upset makes a bond between you. (I even did that for Aunt Anne when I told her that Daddy had come home on the train.) It was getting so that there were some problems I could take to her better than to Mother, because we weren't so close. It made my world larger — more certain. I knew that Mother wouldn't mind, in theory, although she might be hurt in practice.

It's strange when someone you thought was a fool turns out not to be. Ideas about people change a lot as you grow older. It isn't the people that change, it's you. Sometimes you have been the fool.

Of course, both Mother and Aunt Anne saw things as grown-ups, which was a drawback. What's really needed as you grow older is someone your own age.

"It's hard to know —" said Mother.

"I'll meet Priscilla," I said, "because she'll be looking for me. I'll help her pick out the invitations anyway. Then I'll go home with her and tell Aunt Anne no thank you about the party. Then I'll come back here and read and read and read."

It sounded so simple. But I could see that Mother was going to have herself a bad afternoon.

"Anyway," she said, "you'll have a chance to do something about Peter."

She had no idea how right she was.

At four thirty sharp I walked past the

jewelry store and squinted into the window of the bookstore between the fake-fuzzy poinsettias and the gaudy gift-wrapped packages. I could see Priscilla in the back of the store, looking through the cards. I thought that I would help her pick out the card and while we were walking to her house I would explain that I didn't think I would be giving the party with her. Naturally she wouldn't understand, but I hardly thought either she or Aunt Anne would care. Asking me was just a nice gesture.

I was in the mood to get things accomplished. I decided that while I was in the bookstore I might as well get a book about football players for Peter and that would be the end of it. (It's odd how you express yourself sometimes.)

The snow was old and gray. It had been around too long. I wished we'd have a good thaw and wash it all away and start over. I scuffled my feet along the dreary, slushy sidewalk toward the door of the bookstore. I was reaching for the door when I felt two warm hands cover my eyes.

"Guess who?" said the most familiar voice in my world.

It wasn't too hard. "Hi," I said.

"I called your house and your mother said you'd be here at four thirty," said Peter, all happy smiles.

Thanks a lot, Mother, I thought.

From the way he acted I could tell that he had decided to overlook my unfortunate attitude about Dido and Aeneas.

"Have you got my present yet?" he asked.

How like Peter! Anyone would know you

shouldn't ask a thing like that. Whatever small particle of joy I might have had in buying something for him was removed with that question. But Peter could never leave anything to the imagination. What came into his head went out his mouth.

"No," I said, wearily. "I haven't got you anything yet." It wasn't his fault, but I wished he could be different, more like . . . but there was no use wishing.

He put his hands on my shoulders and steered me sideways, away from the bookstore window to the jewelry store alongside it.

"This give you any ideas?" he asked, arching his eyebrows.

In front of me, in the case, were row upon row of shining silver ID bracelets. So that was it. Mother was right. I felt the bump of the old wire Turk's Head under my glove. Something more permanent to take its place. With both our names. One for each of us. Shining silver shackles.

I thought of a hundred gifts that I had given. A woven potholder for Grammy. A ceramic ashtray for Mother. A dollar-fifty watch for Dad. A pair of mittens with dropped stitches for a friend. Always my wish to give was greater and the love that went with it was greater than the poor object could possibly show.

With Peter my wish to give was less than the object he wanted from me. The kind of love he wanted didn't go with it. The bracelet would make him too happy. It wasn't honest to have him that happy on my account. I had to refuse.

"Oh, Peter," I said, leaning my head against the glass. "I can't —"

"They aren't expensive," he said, bumbling down the wrong path entirely. "I could even —"

"No!" I said. I started to shiver.

He would even help me buy it for him! Peter was getting bigger and bigger in this relationship and I was getting smaller and smaller. I had to hold my ground somewhere or I'd vanish entirely.

"Peter," I said, "there's something we had better talk about." My voice must have been quite loud, because two lady shoppers turned their heads to look.

I didn't know how to express myself. "What I want to say is — I need more freedom. I mean sometimes I might not want to go to the football game." I felt small, but defiant.

"Gosh!" he said. Yellow light from the jewelry store window slanted across his surprised face. "I thought you liked football."

"I do," I said.

"Then where do you want to go?" he asked.

"I don't want to go *any*where," I said.

I could see that he didn't know whether to be hurt or not.

"I might just want to stay home and read," I said. "I get sick of going to so many things."

"You're getting just like you used to be," he said, frowning.

That was exactly it. He said it right. I felt the clot of unhappiness dissolve. I had told him and I could go. "That's how I want to be," I said. "The way I used to be. I'm glad you understand. It used to be fun. So we'll agree to give each other some little thing," I said. "OK?" I turned to go. "I have to meet Priscilla —"

He caught my wrist. His fingers were strong. I couldn't pull loose. "No!" he said. "It's not OK!"

"Let me go!" I said. "Get your hands off me!"

People were really staring, slowing down to watch us, but I didn't care.

"If you can't let me be the way I want to be you'd better forget about me," I shouted.

I looked at his face and I wished I hadn't.

"Peter," I said, in a tight broken voice. "It isn't your fault. I don't want you to feel bad about it. It isn't anything you did or . . . anyone else. It's just . . . me. I hope you find a much nicer girl . . . that's always like . . . you want her to be."

I looked down at my wrist, which he was still holding, and I said to him nicely and quietly, "Please, Peter, please let me go."

"Jo —" he begged. It was a plea. For me to say I was sorry. Yield. Dissolve into tears. Do things his way. Give in completely. Because boy-pride, man-pride, would never allow him to budge an inch.

I twisted my wrist. It hurt, but I wrenched myself suddenly free and walked with a straight back and a high head into the bookstore.

He didn't follow me. Not Peter. With Peter quits was quits. The end. Finis.

Finished, that was. Starting right that minute, I thought, I'd as soon forget all the Latin

I ever knew. Especially the poetry.

In my head I still heard his voice, Jo, echoing Jo, echoing Jo —

What would I do next? What would I do about the classes we had together? The parties we were going to? What would I do?

"May I help you?" asked the store lady.

"I guess not," I said.

Nobody could help me. Like after Grammy died.

All the good things during the year were because of Peter. A whole new group of girls started to include me, first because they wanted Peter along and then because they got to like me. And Peter helped me with the math until I found that I could do it by myself.

And what would Peter do? With me to back him up he got so that he didn't take any guff at all from his father. Like the time at the dog show when Dr. Stern took him to the hospital in Greenwich because I insisted. Or if Peter felt like translating Latin poetry instead of doing chemistry he just plonked the old Virgil down on the living-room floor and whipped out the rhyming dictionary. Dr. Stern had even become grudgingly proud of it.

We had been doing everything together for a year, just a year, since the last Christmas Get-Together. Oh, Peter —

I still heard that Jo —. Nobody else called me Jo. I knew I wouldn't get it out of my head until some other voice took its place.

"Priscilla," I said, in a thick voice.

She was still at the Christmas card rack. After that eternity. I had noticed her at four thirty. But the clock said only four forty-five.

"Hi," she said. cheerfully. "I looked at them. They're all dreadful."

"It's all dreadful," I echoed, not sure what she was talking about.

We walked past shelves of paperbacks.

"You look funny," she said. "Do you feel all right?"

"All right," I said. My mind was numb and I couldn't think straight. I couldn't remember why we were in the store.

I followed her to the table. There were two chairs in front of it so we both sat down. There were black albums, open, with white folded-out invitations.

Oh yes, the party. But how could I go to the party when I had broken up with Peter? Oh yes, Mother said I didn't have to go to the party. My head was swimming. I was shaking as though I was outside, but it was warm in the store. I felt woozy, so I took off my gloves and passed my hand over my forehead.

Priscilla's exclamation frightened me. "Jose!" she said. "What happened to your wrist? It looks horrible!"

There was a long scrape mark on the white inside skin of my wrist. Blood had smeared and dried. The yellow Turk's Head was gone.

I remembered the sudden sting when I wrenched free of Peter. I felt dizzy and sick and I swayed in my chair.

"You're sick," said Priscilla. "I'm taking you home."

"I'm not sick," I said. "I just wish I were dead." I leaned my forehead on my hand.

"Peter?" she asked. She looked at me curiously.

I nodded.

"When?"

I couldn't answer.

"Just now?" she asked.

I nodded.

"What a dirty thing to do to you," she exploded. "Two days before Christmas! That no-good —"

"I did it to him," I managed to say. "I told him I was tired of being pushed around. And the trouble is . . . I'm gl-ad." I started to cry.

Priscilla didn't say anything. Like Aunt Anne, she's good at letting people cry. The only sound was the musical tinkle of her silver bracelets.

"I expect you did the right thing," she said, after a while, looking down at her folded hands. "It never works out when one person dominates the other and makes all the decisions."

I wondered who she was thinking of. Her face was pinched and wistful. She waited kindly while I found a handkerchief.

"Let me help you pick out the invitations," I said, wiping my eyes, trying to be cheerful. I didn't want to spoil it for her, her party when her college friends were home on vacation; but I was dying to get done so that I could tell Aunt Anne I wasn't going and run home to the seclusion of my room. "I really feel fine," I said.

"In a way, that's a shame," she said. "For

a minute there I thought you might be coming down with something conveniently lingering — like the two-week flu. But I guess there's no way out of it."

"What do you mean?" I asked, startled. "Don't you want a New Year's Eve party?"

She said a syllable in French that I was sure was a dirty word.

"Priscilla!" I said.

I was shocked. Not by the word, but by Priscilla not wanting a New Year's Eve party. I looked at her closely. What had happened? When? I couldn't possibly ask.

She turned a page in the album. "How about this one?" she said, pointing to a card. "It's not too awful."

"But we won't have the party!" I exclaimed. "You just said so. *I* don't want one. I was planning to go home with you and tell your mother exactly that."

Was I relieved! Priscilla could tell Aunt Anne for both of us and I could go straight home and collapse. I got my wraps together.

"Oh, we'll have to have it," she said. "I couldn't tell them I don't want a party."

"Of course you could," I said, standing, looking down at her.

"I'm not like you, Jose," she said. "I can't tell people off honestly and decently." She covered her face with her hands. "I could never do what you did with Peter. I'd do it some mean, sneaky way. Like through a friend. Or I'd pretend it was all his fault."

"I would despise myself if I pretended," I said. "It's kinder to be honest and say what you mean out straight." I was getting some thoughts together. "Like — now Peter knows the real reason, which is my difficult personality. He doesn't have to go through any long nastiness of wondering if there is some other boy, or if he did anything wrong. He can blame me. He even knows I hope he finds . . . another girl."

I looked down at my still throbbing wrist. It felt raw and naked. "It's like a . . . clean cut that starts to heal right away, without a scar," I explained to myself.

"I couldn't," she said.

I had almost forgotten about Priscilla. Everything was solved as far as I was concerned. What was she fussing about?

"It's easy," I said, as though I were explaining to a child. "You go home and say, 'Mother —' "

"I call her 'Mums,' " she said weakly.

"Well, start calling her *Mother*!" I said, irritated. " 'Mother, I certainly appreciate you and Dad wanting to give me the party, but Josie and I have decided that we are all tired out from school and that we'd really enjoy the party a whole lot more if we took a rain check until spring vacation. I know you won't mind and we certainly appreciate the thought.' "

I slammed the invitation book closed. "And when you tell her, try not to be the one that starts the yelling," I said, as an afterthought. "It puts you at a disadvantage."

"Oh, Jose," she said, gripping my hand. It was the one that hurt, but I didn't flinch. "Come home with me."

I didn't want to. I was exhausted. I thought

about my quiet room and D'Artagnan and my green comforter. I didn't mind telling Aunt Anne, "No thank you," but Priscilla would still have to do it for herself.

"Jose?" she pleaded.

Looking at her I saw that going to her house meant more to her than staying at my house meant to me. For the second time in one day I was in the position to do something important for someone, and this time I could do it with my whole heart.

"I guess . . . I could," I said. I was surprised how much better saying it made me feel.

"I might even make you a dress," she said, under her breath.

"I'd like that," I said shyly. I tried to push away the sudden terror that she'd heard the nasty things I'd said in school. "Could you make my dress with a long skinny hot dog smiling across my stomach?" I asked in a rush.

She looked at me pointedly. "I was thinking of making you one out of a burlap bag," she said.

I blushed crimson. It wasn't easy to apologize, because when I'd said those things I'd really meant them. But I managed. "Priscilla," I said, "I'm sorry I ever —"

"I asked for it," she interrupted quickly. "Would you like ketchup or mustard on your dog?"

"Both!" I said.

"Don't you think it might be a little —" she paused.

"De trop?" I asked.

We both laughed.

"I'll be proud to wear it any way you fix it," I said.

Sixteen scrappy years — forgotten, wiped out, obliterated.

"Mums will think we're upstairs writing out invitations," she giggled. "And actually we'll be making your dress."

"None of that!" I said, pointing my finger at her. "No backsliding. The minute we walk in the front door I'm saying, 'Aunt Anne, Priscilla has something to tell you.' And you're telling her or I'm leaving."

Priscilla groaned, but she straightened her back and marched resolutely toward the door.

Aunt Anne might even be relieved, I thought. Not a bad Christmas present, an independent daughter.

Peter might be relieved too, once it stopped hurting. He knew it had to end sometime. It was only for a while. He had even told me so, the way Hemingway said it.

But this wasn't such a tragedy. In our own fashion we had given each other quite a lot, the year we had together. I ended it when it was ready to be over, while things were still good, without deceit, so that he had an untarnished memory of the things we did together. I gave him the best that I honestly could.

Giving might be a privilege, as Mother tried to tell me. But giving without an equal return ends up not working. Aunt Anne and Priscilla. Peter and me.

What does work is when you offer your best to someone who needs it and she offers you her best in return. Like a shift with a smiling hot dog in exchange for some sturdy moral support in the ring. Priscilla and me.

I sighed with relief as I trudged past the Christmas-lit houses with Priscilla beside me. Warmth and well-being and Christmas comfort flooded through me. Everything was settled!

10

The Eye of the Beholder

Everything was not settled. In fact it turned out to be the most *un*settled winter of my whole life.

For one thing, from the very moment that Priscilla and I patched things up, we started pulling hard as a team. The new lineup threw Mother and Aunt Anne off balance. They found the two of us impossible to deal with; we played them, one against the other, shamelessly.

The other thing . . . the other thing I promised myself all winter not to really think about until I could be at the shore again. Even while it got bigger and bigger, I had to keep it out of the thinking part of my mind until I could be there. Because it was at the shore that I could see things most clearly.

It was like the time when I made myself not think about the lamp and the frightful scene with Dad. Because the thoughts were so painful.

But this time, the thoughts contained so much joy I was almost afraid of them.

Actually Priscilla's graduation took up most of the last half of the winter. The second weekend in May I gave a lunch party for Priscilla and a few of her good friends. We had it outdoors in our backyard on a mild spring day with the fragrance of daffodils and hyacinths all about us. Beyond the yard distant trees were puffs of soft green. Everything was new and fresh and beginning, but sadness was very close because the girls knew how soon it would be goodbye for good. I almost wished I hadn't done it, but I knew it was good that I had.

The last month of school, from the middle of May on, was totally frantic. After graduation Priscilla and I thought Mother and Aunt Anne would be delighted to see the end of us. But even though they were exhausted, we had the devil's own time persuading them to let us drive up to the shore together a day early to open the house. Anything we did on wheels terrified them.

So it was, "What do you think about it, Anne? I hate to be a spoilsport, *but* —" and "Well, they really deserve a treat for being such good girls, *but* on the other hand —"

They couldn't get together with an outright no, but we never managed a clear-cut yes, even dealing with them separately. Arguing about it took up most of my spare time and kept my mind occupied. Priscilla finally thought of working through Uncle Jack. He became unglued quite readily and the opposition folded.

Uncle Jack drove us as far as Boston and we all spent the night in a motel on Beacon Street. We dragged him all over Boston that night (though most of the places we wanted to go he wouldn't take us) and we put him on the train for home the next morning. He waved at me from the seat in the smoker and mopped his bald head with his handkerchief as the train pulled out of South Station. Priscilla and I looked at each other and grinned. Free!

Priscilla had had her senior license for two months (in a year I would have mine). There were a few hair-raising moments on the Maine Turnpike and a bitter argument about lighting cigarettes at sixty miles an hour, but we arrived at the shore safely, in time for lunch.

Mother and Aunt Anne and Paul were to drive up the following evening. Dad and Uncle Jack planned to take the first plane on Saturday. Just like every other summer. Almost.

Even after a winter of being shut up, the house didn't smell musty, but deliciously of dry wood and pine needles. Priscilla went downtown in the car to buy food for the kitchen cabinets and I aired out closets and opened windows and made beds and shook mothballs out of blankets.

For a long time, as we went about our business, we walked quietly back and forth past Grammy's door, not opening it.

I remembered how one of the first things Daddy said — afterward — was, "Who shall have Grammy's room at the shore?" and Aunt Anne said, "Josie, of course."

So I would sleep in the big four-poster bed

with the fluffy blanket and the white candle-wick bedspread; I would use the oval mirror and the dresser with the marble top when I was at the shore. I was to have her scrapbooks, too.

We had every other room done and finally Priscilla said gruffly, "I'll take her things out and put them in boxes and stack them in the shed for our mothers to go over, if you don't want to."

And I said, "Maybe you'd better."

It's strange how things work out. I used to hate sharing a room with Priscilla, but for the first time, when I didn't have to, it would have been good to. Priscilla and I weren't going to be seeing much of each other any more.

I did a final check in Paul's room. It looked too clean and bare. I missed the usual collection of dried eyes. In another week, I knew, every windowsill would be a happy clutter of crumpled seaweed and shells, and the floor would be gritty with sand from blue-jean cuffs and unemptied sneakers.

Paul still had summer after summer at the shore. He was just beginning his best summers — and I was just ending. I promised myself that I would always come back for part of every summer.

I leaned out Paul's window so that I could look up and down the familiar shoreline, bright in the noon sunshine. The trees on the hill behind the beach were a delicate spring green and the sweet smell of privet mingled with the salt breeze. I felt such a sudden charge of happiness that I could hardly catch my breath. I couldn't wait any longer.

"Priscillaaaa!" I shouted, turning from the window.

"Here," she answered joyfully.

I found her wiping off refrigerator shelves with washing soda. She looked desperately like Aunt Anne, but I knew she wasn't like her, really.

"Would you mind if I went down to the beach for a minute?" I asked.

"Course not," she said. "I'm perfectly happy as long as I don't have Mother standing over me, telling me which way to fold the dust cloth . . . I'm going to miss her," she said, suddenly, turning to me wide-eyed, with a hint of tears.

"You'll be fine," I said. "You'll see."

I knew it would be chilly on the beach, so I took my old sailing jacket off the hook behind the kitchen door where it had been hanging since September.

"Priscilla," I said, making myself ask the question that I hadn't been able to get around to on the way up in the car. "Are you going to stay at the shore all summer?"

"Until we go to Europe in August," said Priscilla. "Why do you ask?" She paused to look at me.

"Oh, I don't know," I said, shrugging casually.

"Aren't *you?*" she asked.

I shrugged again.

"How queer of you," she said. "What are you going to do? The shore has always been your whole summer —"

I ran away from her questions, out the back screen door and down the steps to the meadow and under the arch of oaks and along the pathway to the beach.

There it was!

The fresh onshore breeze had kicked up a cheerful chop. Sunlight sparkled on the wave tips and white flecks of foam flew up the shingle.

I threw myself full length on the sun-warm sand and from the pocket of my dress I pulled the letter.

I had folded it and unfolded it so often that the fold lines were almost worn through. For the moment I didn't open it. I buried my head on my arms and closed my eyes. Finally I could allow myself to think . . .

. . . back to the December evening when I had just broken up with Peter and was walking home along the Christmas-lit streets with Priscilla beside me.

As it turned out, Peter had a new girl by New Year's. A good friend of mine, if you please. She had been working on moving in for some time. By the time school started in January there were no hard feelings. In fact, I was able to give her a few friendly tips. Every time I saw Peter all through the spring he chatted cheerfully on about the wonderful times we used to have when we were doing things together. He even took me to another dog show, for old times' sake.

Still, I had had some miserable moments about him. The new coalition with Priscilla was a big help. It got my mind off Peter. We gave Aunt Anne her first taste of trouble that same evening when Priscilla marched resolutely in the front door of her house, flanked by me.

Aunt Anne was watering the philodendrons in the living-room bay window with a copper watering can that had a long spout but didn't look as though it held much water. Priscilla took forever in the coat closet, so I went in with her and gave her an encouraging poke. "Owwww —" she said.

"What did you say, dear?" asked Aunt Anne. "Was it very bad downtown? Did you and Josie manage the invitations?"

"Now," I whispered to Priscilla.

Priscilla switched her blond hair from side to side and hung on to the back of an upholstered chair.

"Mother," she began, "I certainly appreciate you and Dad wanting to give me the party —" She turned her head quickly to see how I thought she was doing. I nodded approval.

"That's all right, Sweet," said Aunt Anne. "Dads and I are happy to do it for you."

"But Josie and I are all tired out from school —" Priscilla went on.

"Poor babies," said Aunt Anne. "Of course you are." The gold bracelets on her wrists tinkled as she parted the heart-shaped leaves to find the soil. "You deserve the most devastating, exciting, glamorous vacation for your senior year."

I was afraid Priscilla was going to fizzle out. Aunt Anne came over to her and patted her arm soothingly. "Leave everything to Mums," she said. "I'm going to fix it all up for my good girls. You won't need to think of a thing but parties."

I got the surprise of my life. Priscilla suddenly cut loose from the script.

"Mother, I'm having a hard time making it clear to you that I don't want a party," said Priscilla. She was trembling slightly.

Aunt Anne looked wispy and a trifle confused. "A theater group?" she asked.

Priscilla shook her head.

"Something at a supper club in town?"

"NO PARTY!" said Priscilla.

"But child, you haven't been to a single social event since you got back from Paris," said Aunt Anne, looking at her closely with a little puzzled frown.

"And I don't plan to go to a single social event this whole vacation," said Priscilla in a loud defiant tone. "You can't make me!"

Her words hung in the air. Aunt Anne studied her face. The way she looked reminded me of the way she had glanced at me in the car on the way to the Spring Get-Together, when I was wildly romanticizing about Henry. She must have had an inkling of trouble.

The business of no one saying anything unnerved me. In my family everyone would have been yelling at once and slamming doors by that time. Finally Aunt Anne spoke.

"You met someone in Europe," she said, with quiet authority.

Priscilla's face turned scarlet.

Aunt Anne's puckered up. "Baby!" she cried and burst into tears.

Priscilla started to cry too.

I remembered her thin face and the dark circles under her eyes when she showed up at the shore in August; I began to feel weepy myself, not to mention a bit unnecessary. "I'll be upstairs in Priscilla's room," I announced, loudly, marching up the stairs. I don't think either one of them heard me.

Priscilla's room had changed since I last saw it. There were travel posters of France on all four walls. On one side, against the wall, there was a long table with a sewing machine and bolts of yard goods stacked high. I tried out some of the different colors in front of her full-length mirror. I was getting to the point where I liked to be looked at. Amazing how you change between fourteen and sixteen! I was an eyeful!

I chose a piece of vivid yellow material that had already been cut and pulled it over my head. It hung loose at the sides. I was admiring myself extravagantly when Priscilla opened the door.

"That looks nice," she said. Her eyes were red, but they were calm and peaceful.

"Would you like me to powder your nose?" I asked, sympathetically, so that she would know it mattered to me.

"Mother already did," she said, rubbing her swollen eyelids.

"Is she mad?" I asked.

Priscilla shook her head. *"Tout comprendre, c'est tout pardonner."*

"To understand all . . ." I translated haltingly, "is to forgive all."

She nodded.

I decided that it was the same in any language.

I thought she might not be in the mood for working on the shift, so I started to pull it off over my head.

"Wait a minute," she said, making her voice businesslike and cheerful. "Let's try basting it on." She threaded a big-eyed needle with coarse black thread. "We have a few minutes before dinner. Dad should be along soon."

She ran the thread skillfully up each side seam. "There." She broke the thread and knotted it.

"It's a little tight," I said. "I don't think I can get it off."

Downstairs the front door opened and slammed and we heard a male voice. Voices, it turned out.

"Oh, dear," I said. "Uncle Jack! What'll I do?"

"Priscilla —" Uncle Jack called up the stairway. "Sweetie, come see who I brought home for you."

"I can't get this thing off," I said, struggling.

"Don't pull at it," Priscilla ordered. "You can wear it to dinner. Mother won't mind as long as we are *en famille*." She was halfway down the stairs.

Oh, well, I thought, so what. I ran after her.

En famille was the last thing we were to be. I paused and looked down on two up-turned faces. Uncle Jack's, familiar, round, smile-wrinkled, comfortable, and — my mouth went dry and my stomach knotted up — Uncle Jack's cousin on his mother's side, my ever-lasting shame, Henry Bassett.

In panic I backed up the stairs above the

landing where no one could see me. There I stopped and looked down on the scene below.

"Found him in Grand Central," said Uncle Jack, genially. "On his way down from Cambridge. And he wasn't going to call. Didn't want to bother us. Think of that. Flying to Denver tomorrow morning. Right, boy?"

"I have to get back," said Henry, nervously adjusting his tie.

"Oh, I wish we'd known you were coming," said Aunt Anne in a thin little voice. I knew she was worrying about me.

"I don't want to put you out," said Henry. "I can only stay a few minutes."

He was looking uneasily at Priscilla. I remembered how Aunt Anne had tried to get him to escort Priscilla around whenever she thought she could catch up with him. It struck me funny, thinking how he must have spent at least one thoroughly unwilling weekend at Priscilla's house. Because he had obligations. And Uncle Jack had caught him again.

Henry didn't know that he needn't worry about Priscilla or Aunt Anne any more. He stood on the doormat, squirming inside, I was sure.

"Hi, Henry," said Priscilla, without a spark of interest or enthusiasm. "How's school?"

"OK," he said, matching her flat tone.

I remembered him as looking older. He didn't seem any different than a lot of boys I knew. Except that you couldn't call him a boy any more.

"M.I.T., isn't it?" said Priscilla.

"Yeah," said Henry.

No one was paying any attention to me and

I was surprised to find that every scrap of nervousness had vanished. I looked Henry over objectively. He hadn't grown taller, but his shoulders under his tweed jacket seemed heavier. His face was still serious, a little longer and thinner, but friendly. I suddenly felt sorry for him. Uncle Jack had dragged him all the way out to the suburbs and not one person in the house was the least bit glad to see him.

"Oh," said Priscilla, remembering me behind her. "Have you met my cousin Josie?" She frowned. I could see that she honestly couldn't remember whether I had or hadn't. It was unimportant to her.

I guessed that Aunt Anne had never told her about my miserable experience with Henry. Looking at him now, the whole thing made me want to laugh. I could make quite a story of it, to tell Priscilla, to cheer her up, to make her laugh with me. What a moon-struck child I had been!

"I'm not sure I have met her," said Henry, coming up a step and holding out his hand. "Come out into the light, Josie, where a man can see you."

Hearing him say my name gave me prickles. But I wasn't blushing. I came down the stairs and offered my hand like a queen.

Aunt Anne was standing very still.

"I think I do remember you," he said, slowly. "Yes. I met you a couple of years ago — at some kind of a dance. You were much . . . ah . . . younger. Just a little . . ." He didn't know how to end it and I had no plans to help him. I relished his confusion.

"We talked about boats on the porch," he continued, speaking faster. "About Cuttyhunk." His eyes lit up suddenly and began to laugh, the way I remembered. It gave me a jolt inside. He looked me up and down. "You *must* remember," he insisted.

"I don't know," I said, pretending to give the matter earnest thought. "I'm afraid I don't." I frowned. "But then, of course, I talk to a great many people, and frequently about boats. It's one of my favorite subjects."

I was stunned to find myself with the situation — and Henry — in the palm of my hand. It was time for some fun.

"How do you like this color, Aunt Anne?" I asked, deliberately turning my back on Henry. I put a hand on one hip and the other flat against the back of my head and honkytonked across the living room, taking little mincing steps.

I knew the shift was shapely.

"Don't you think it brings me out?" I asked Aunt Anne, popping my eyes at her wickedly.

She let out a big breath. She was looking pretty pale.

Priscilla stared. I wondered if she'd had a sudden memory of how I'd danced with Henry. I thought maybe Henry was remembering too.

"Do you always wear your clothes inside out, Josie?" asked Henry, following me across the living room, trying to attract my attention.

"Only on odd Thursdays," I answered witheringly.

"Did I hear you invite me to spend the night, Anne?" asked Henry. "But of course I'd love to. It's ever so thoughtful of you and I accept with pleasure."

"No . . . uh . . . yes," said Aunt Anne. "Yes . . . of course." I could see that the evening was reducing her to an emotional jelly.

All evening I felt Priscilla watching me and Henry. I knew that she wanted urgently to talk to me. Later, when we'd gone to bed, she was able to. It's always easier to talk in the dark because you don't have to see the person you're talking to.

She wanted to talk about Paris. She told me that when she arrived she found she was to have charge of an eleven-year-old girl named Annette. Annette went to boarding school in Switzerland during the winter and had come home for the summer holidays. It was a motherless household. There was an indulgent old family housekeeper. The father was away on business a good deal; the rest of the time he was occupied with affairs (so to speak) of his own.

Priscilla had settled into a routine of English and mathematics in the morning and tennis in the afternoon with little Annette, when brother Jacques (age twenty) turned up home from college. When Jacques saw Priscilla he decided to stay. He found an undemanding summer job in Paris.

No one had told the guidance counselor at school about Jacques. The housekeeper was indulgent; the father was occupied. Priscilla learned flawless French (among other things) from Jacques. And Annette learned to amuse herself (which, as it turned out, she managed quite capably).

By the end of August things were getting serious. Priscilla couldn't tell me without breaking down, and my French wasn't that good, but I gathered that Jacques couldn't let her go without some sort of an understanding. He gave her, not a ring, but a beautiful garnet pendant that had been in his mother's family since before Napoleon. She kept it under her pillow and she showed it to me. It was the loveliest thing I ever saw. A blood-red teardrop.

"Oh, Priscilla," I said. "What will you do?"

"I don't know," she said. "I love Paris. It's me. More than here. But I'm too young. We're both too young. I'm scared. I'll have to send it back." Her fingers tightened on the stone. "But I ca-an't."

"One way to find out," I said, slowly, thinking. "You could study at the Sorbonne next winter. Instead of junior college."

She gasped. "That's just what Mother said!" She jumped out of bed. "Do you think I could?" she asked. "What do I do? Who do I write?"

"Not in the middle of the night, Priscilla," I said.

But I thought she might as well. I knew I wasn't going to get much sleep anyway. It had been such an emotional day. So after we wrote her letter to the Sorbonne and after she had written to Jacques, we went downstairs very quietly and got a potato and pierced my ears. After that we were able to sleep.

Henry managed to miss plane after plane the next day. I finally agreed to have lunch

209

with him in New York, just so that he'd get going.

His family wasn't too pleased, but he talked them into letting him spend New Year's weekend with Aunt Anne and Uncle Jack. He called me from Denver first thing Christmas morning and asked to have New Year's Eve with me. I still have the camellias.

He wrote during the winter term and he wanted me to go up to Cambridge for a weekend, but Mother said that was out.

The only time I saw him after New Year's was during spring vacation, one evening between planes and trains. He took me to the Spring Get-Together. He said, "Do you have to go to that thing?" and I said, "Mother paid for it," so he said, "Back to our old stamping ground," and I chuckled to myself. He took me in Uncle Jack's car. That was in March.

I lifted my head from the hot sand and unfolded the letter:

Dear Josie—
Pages of calculus ahead, but I can't get my mind on it until I write.

Good news! You know about my job at Columbia during July and August. But hear this! Dad has chartered a ketch for the last two weeks in June. The first port of call will be your summer place. If we make Dad comfortable we may never get any further.

You and I can try your sloop. Yes? Day after day!

Josie, we have so much to talk about. I have something to ask you. We have this summer only once. Do you have to spend all of it at the shore? Would you spend part of it with your father in Westchester? I know what I'm asking.

The rest will have to wait until I see you.

Soon!
Henry

I folded the letter and put it back into the envelope and tried to fit it into my jacket pocket. Something interfered. I reached in and my fingers found the stone, round and pure white. It had been in my pocket over the winter, forgotten during the rush of packing those two days after Grammy's wild sail in September.

Seeing it took me back. So that I was fourteen again, when the hardest day for me was in September, the last day before we left the shore. It was as though I was looking through the wrong end of a telescope; within the confines of its tiny circle I looked back on a different self, a far-off place, a distant time.

I scooped up a handful of sand and let the dry grains slip onto the stone and bounce off. It made me smile to remember Henry's physical reflections about the properties of a sphere the night we met. Drawn inward, exposing the least possible of itself; secret, safe, inviolate. That was how *I* was! I laughed out loud.

What was the fun of living inside of a sphere?

Outside there was Peter. *Ave atque vale,* Peter. Hail and farewell.

Priscilla and Aunt Anne. I was there when

Aunt Anne gave Priscilla her graduation present. It was a gold chain. As I watched her walk up to the platform in her white graduation dress, I saw that she was wearing the blood-red teardrop at her throat. I suddenly understood — when the speaker said that commencement was not an end, but a beginning —

These were my fools. Suffer them gladly?

There aren't any fools, I thought. What is real, like beauty, is in the eye of the beholder, and you take it with you wherever you go.

I picked up the stone again, cradled it in my hand. It had contained for me a place, and also a period of time, summers until this one. But the place and the time were a part of me now. I didn't need to cling to them any more. The shore was *only* a place; the period of time was over.

I was free to go.

Dad would be astonished when I showed up in Westchester again and told him that I wanted to spend the better part of the summer with him. (I, who would never give up the shore for anyone.) I expected that I could get a daytime job at the pool, baby sitting, while the mothers played tennis.

I felt a second surge of joy and jumped to my feet.

Out near the channel markers, beyond the safety of the harbor beacon, I saw black, glossy humps curving against the white caps. Porpoises! I knew how they must feel, leaping through the water. What reason could there be for a porpoise to jump like that except that he was so bursting with joy that the water couldn't hold him and he had to hurl himself into a new, untried element?

I ran to the water's edge.

The sun made a dazzling roadway as the waves marched shoreward; each triangle wave tip brought a sparkling diamond straight to my feet.

Who needs stones? I thought. I sent my stone zinging out over the glittering path and watched it drop with a cheerful plop into the water to generate ever-widening and expanding concentric circles.

Into the pocket where the stone had been, I stuffed the letter.